ALSO BY LAURA VAN DEN BERG

*What the World Will Look Like When All the Water
Leaves Us*

# THE ISLE OF YOUTH

# THE ISLE OF YOUTH

STORIES

LAURA VAN DEN BERG

FARRAR, STRAUS AND GIROUX   NEW YORK

Farrar, Straus and Giroux
18 West 18th Street, New York 10011

Printed in the United States of America
First edition, 2013

Library of Congress Cataloging-in-Publication Data
Van den Berg, Laura.
    [Short stories. Selections]
    The Isle of Youth : stories / Laura Van den Berg. — First edition.
      pages   cm
    ISBN 978-0-374-17723-2 (pbk.)—ISBN 978-0-374-71061-3 (ebook)
    I.   Title.

    PS3622.A58537 I85 2013
    813'.6—dc23

                                                    2013022588


Designed by Abby Kagan

Farrar, Straus and Giroux books may be purchased for educational, business,
or promotional use. For information on bulk purchases, please contact the
Macmillan Corporate and Premium Sales Department at 1-800-221-7945,
extension 5442, or write to specialmarkets@macmillan.com.

www.fsgbooks.com
www.twitter.com/fsgbooks • www.facebook.com/fsgbooks

10  9  8  7  6  5  4  3  2  1

FOR PAUL, *my isle*

I felt I was playing a part in a movie with a plot unknown to me.

—YOKO TAWADA, *The Naked Eye*

# CONTENTS

I LOOKED FOR YOU,

I CALLED YOUR NAME

The first thing that went wrong was the emergency landing. My husband and I were both reading *In Flight Magazine* and enjoying the complimentary wine in first class—I'd never flown first class before, but it was our honeymoon and we thought that was what we were supposed to do; drink in the daytime, luxuriate in our good fortune—when the plane lurched and oxygen masks fell from the ceiling and a passenger in the back screamed. We didn't know it then, but the pilot was already steering the plane toward an empty brown field, preparing for our descent.

The landing itself was terrifying: a hard, screeching wallop that knocked us around in our seats. Wine spilled in our laps. Bags overturned and people's possessions spread into the aisle. My husband elbowed me right in the nose and I tasted blood in my mouth. When we finally stopped, the flight attendants, all of them leggy and red-lipped, applauded, as though the emergency landing had been performed for our amusement. I unbuckled my seatbelt and cupped my nose, stunned silent by the pain.

"The seatbelt sign is still on," my husband said, resting a hand on my back.

I leaned forward, away from his touch. These were the kinds of moments that had been recently giving me pause. *We're new at this*, I kept telling myself, but there was no denying that I was often confounded by his priorities.

I sat up and touched my nose. It felt swollen. I looked down at the pool of red in my lap and dipped my pinkie finger into the wine. We thought we had overcome the worst, having endured the flight from Newark to Houston, the ten-hour trip to Buenos Aires, and the connection to El Calafate Airport in Patagonia, but all I could think about was how wrong we'd been.

My husband continued staring at the illuminated seatbelt sign. My entire face hummed with pain.

"It doesn't matter anymore," I said to him, licking the wine off my fingertip. "We're on the ground now."

Within an hour, black buses arrived and carried us away from the field and the airplane sitting uselessly in it. A representative from the airline came too, a young man dressed in a pinstriped suit. It was a mechanical error, we were told. The injuries had all been minor: a woman cradling her forearm, a man with a gash on his cheek, my banged nose. A full refund would be forthcoming. The man passed out little cakes in plastic wrappers to the passengers.

In the bus, my husband took my hand, but let go when he realized my fingers were sticky with wine. He pulled hand sanitizer from his bag and squirted a dollop into his palm.

"What are you sanitizing?" I said. "You just touched me."

"If you'd read the statistics on how many people don't wash their hands after using public toilets, you'd be sanitizing too."

I went to the tiny bathroom in the back of the bus and looked in the mirror. My nose was swollen, the nostrils crusted with dried blood. I tore a piece of toilet paper in half and wedged the white clumps into my nose. As I made my way back to my seat, a few of the other passengers stared.

I looked out at the fields dotted with sheep, their coats gray and shaggy. We passed a stone church and a woman selling paper-wrapped fish from a roadside stand. We were outside San Antonio Oeste, where our resort, Las Grutas, was located, on the San Matías Gulf. This was in the province of Río Negro, the northern edge of Patagonia. As we drew closer to Las Grutas, the landscape got rockier; we went by a row of hulking granite formations, reddish in color, like a miniature mountain range. It was January when we left our home in Philadelphia, but in Patagonia it was summer, the weather warm and breezy.

When we finally arrived at the resort, a tall white building with arched windows, we learned we'd been upgraded to a suite, courtesy of the airline. In the lobby, we passed the manager's office. The door was open. A TV was mounted on the wall and tuned to the news. I glimpsed a reporter standing by the white nose of an airplane and paused, but I didn't understand enough Spanish to make out what was being said. I'd been practicing Spanish with a Rosetta Stone video, and when I arrived in Patagonia, I was disappointed to learn that I'd retained only a collection of random words, fragments of sentences and thoughts.

From our bedroom, there was a marvelous view of the sea cliffs and the beach beneath them. The sand was powdery and white and marked with dark rocks, including a huge stone in the vague shape of a ship. The tide was going out and every time the waves rolled away they left a sheen on the beach. For the first time since we landed, I felt like everything was going to be okay.

That night, during the cocktail hour held in the lobby, we struck up a conversation with a British couple who were in Patagonia to celebrate their tenth wedding anniversary. Around us waiters in maroon uniforms served pastries with cheese in the center and medio medios, cocktails made of white wine and champagne. Before leaving our room, I'd taken the paper out of my nose and noticed that the skin beneath my eyes had started to darken.

"A decade," the wife kept saying. "Can you believe it?"

"It goes by like that," the husband would add, snapping his fingers.

They were the Humbolts, George and Christina, and they had already been in Patagonia for a week. George was tall and lanky, an overgrown boy, and wore white socks with his sandals, his toes poking over the edges. Christina was petite and graceful. Her blond hair had been gathered into a loose bun, revealing a slender neck wrapped in a fluffy brown scarf.

"It's made from guanaco hair," she said when she caught me eyeing it. "A guanaco is kind of like a llama, but it isn't actually a llama. It just looks like one."

"We got that from a market in San Antonio Oeste," George said.

"You should go this weekend," she said before filling us in on everything else they'd been doing in Patagonia, encouraging scuba diving and bird-watching especially.

"These waters are the warmest in all of Patagonia," she said. "And there are six endemic species of bird in the area."

"Can you name them?" my husband asked.

"Let's see, there's the sandy gallito, the white cachalote, and the rusty monjita," Christina said. "And then there's some kind of warbling finch, the burrowing parrot, and the yellow cardinal, which is endangered."

The men raised their glasses, impressed. Christina shrugged and tucked a loose wave of hair behind her ear. "I read a book," she said.

"Don't forget Iguazú Falls," George said. "You have to take a charter plane, but the hotel will set it all up. They're really something. Taller than Niagara."

"Not another plane," I said, touching my nose.

"Oh, you must go." Christina wrapped her small hand around my forearm. Her fingers were firm and cold. "You really must."

"We'll make the arrangements tomorrow morning. I doubt we'll have two near-death experiences in one trip," my husband said, and everyone laughed but me.

When George wanted to know how we met, my husband explained that it had been at my neighbor's holiday party. It was snowing that night, and I was the only person not wearing some kind of Christmas sweater; my neighbor, for example, had worn a red shirt with little gold bells glued onto her nipples and a Santa hat.

"When I first walked in, I saw her," my husband said, his enthusiasm growing. "I went to the bar and mixed her a drink. I brought it over to her and told her my name and that was that."

George and Christina nodded, then looked at me. "That's right," I said. "He brought me a screwdriver. And then we went out for six months and then he proposed one night, when we were on our way home from a movie. It was raining and he stopped on the sidewalk and asked me right there." I remembered standing under a streetlamp and looking down at his face, his eyelashes thick with rain, and feeling a tremendous surge of hope.

"It was spontaneous," my husband said. "Possibly the first spontaneous thing I've ever done."

"And possibly the last." This time, I was the one trying to make a joke, but no one laughed.

The story we were telling was at once true and not true. The facts were right, but certain details had been omitted. I never brought up my intense dislike for screwdrivers, or said that I drank it only because I had been very lonely that year and didn't want him to stop talking to me. I never brought up all the time I spent in dark movie theaters or playhouses or classical music halls—the hallmarks of my husband's carefully planned dates—trying to understand what, exactly, I felt for him. An attachment, certainly, though I was never sure it was love. But what did it mean to be in love? Maybe all the things people said about falling in love, about the initial torrent of joy, were a lie. And then there was the matter of how my days and weeks and months had become so unexceptional, they were nearly indistinguishable from one another—marked only by my job at a second-rate law firm and the occasional date and watching the weather shift through my apartment windows.

In Philadelphia, I was close to my parents in Bala Cynwyd, where I had grown up, where my twin sister, when we were just four weeks old, had died a silent, inexplicable death in the crib next to mine. I was too young to remember anything about her; as an adult I had tried and tried. Whenever I took the train from Philadelphia to Bala Cynwyd on the weekends, the absent look on my parents' faces—it would appear for only an instant, when I emerged from the crowd outside the station and met their eyes through the car windshield—reminded me of how I had failed to fill my life and my sister's at the same time, a task that had left me with the feeling of always being half-present and half-absent. As the years passed, it became harder to tell the difference between the two, to understand what exactly my capacities were. My husband was an only child. He had come to Philadelphia from Kansas City and saw his parents once a year. He always seemed resolute and sure.

On our dates, I would sit beside him in the dark and gaze at his profile and think all of this through. I was still thinking it through after I moved into his apartment and after we got married. I was still thinking it through as I stood in this hotel lobby in Patagonia, trying to under-stand, a sketch artist attempting to construct a face from disparate descriptions of noses and ears. But these were the kinds of details that could not be spoken of without inflicting real damage.

"Oh, I just love these kinds of stories," Christina said. "Now how are you finding married life?"

"It's nice," I said. "A little confusing at times, but mostly nice." I scratched the side of my nose.

Later that night, when we were back in our room, my husband would tell me how embarrassing it was to hear me describe married life as "confusing." How it made us seem strange and hurt his feelings too. I would point out that I had also used the word "nice," but he would be unmoved, taking a shower that lasted over an hour. But when I'd said it in the hotel lobby, he'd just smiled a flat smile and left to refresh his drink.

Arranging a trip to Iguazú Falls was surprisingly easy. In the morning, a taxi drove us to the airport, where we took a charter plane. During our flight, I never once looked out the window, sitting straight in my seat and trying to ignore the crushing pain in my nose. My husband's annoyance with me had lingered; he'd snapped at me when I was slow going through airport security, and on the plane he scrutinized the Iguazú section in his guidebook, ignoring me completely.

At Iguazú, the guide, a short man with a carefully groomed mustache, picked us up. On the way to the falls, he told us about the legend of their creation: a god had planned to marry a woman, but she loved a mortal man. When she tried to escape with him in a canoe, the god divided the river. The waterfalls were formed and the couple would never stop drowning. The guide told us this story without enthusiasm, never once raising his eyes to meet ours in the rearview. I wondered if the legend was really a legend or just something for the tourists.

"Actually," my husband said, "the falls are the result of a massive volcanic eruption that occurred approximately two hundred thousand years ago."

"Garganta del Diablo," the guide said in response.

"What does that mean?" I whispered to my husband.

"Devil's Throat," he said, pointing to a page in his guidebook.

We entered the falls from the Argentinean town of Puerto Iguazú. The horseshoe-shaped cascades spread across two miles of the Iguazú River, the guide explained as we started our tour on a wood-planked walkway. My husband moved briskly. The guide struggled to keep up, and it wasn't long before I fell behind them both. As we trekked higher, the treetops blended together, making the canopy so dense it obscured the sky. Small brown monkeys swung across the trees. We passed stands of bamboo, orchids, and ceibos, which, my husband called over his shoulder, were the national flower of Argentina. I imagined George and Christina walking this same trail, identifying birds and primates together, reaching down at the same time to touch the velvety leaves of a plant.

When the falls came into view, they were just as spectacular as the Humbolts had said. Water poured over two massive cliffs and pooled in a huge expanse speckled with mossy rocks, as though a lush island had been overtaken by a flood. And then there was the sound, the deep rushing noise that burned away the confusion and the worry. My fingertips tingled and there was a ringing in my ears, but it was pleasant, like distant bells.

"It's the sound of the drowned lovers," the guide said to us. "Time has turned them into something beautiful."

My husband looked at me and slipped his guidebook

into his back pocket. He offered me bug repellent. I let him spray his palms and rub my bare arms and legs. He took his time, making sure the backs of my knees and the insides of my elbows had been covered. His fingertips were cool and I relished the sensation of him touching certain parts of my body—the bones in my ankles—for the very first time. I listened to the falls and wondered if what I was feeling could be called love.

"One of the seven natural wonders of the world," the guide said after we finished.

"Bug spray?" I said, and this time, my husband laughed.

A cloud of turquoise-and-black butterflies swarmed around one of the rocks, touched down for a moment, and then scattered.

"Garganta del Diablo," the guide said again. My husband and I followed him to a footbridge, which, after a great deal of hiking, led us to the Devil's Throat. It was much larger than the others, with jagged rocks jutting through the curtains of water. The sound was deafening.

"The best one," he shouted. "Out of hundreds of falls, this is the best one."

"We're already seeing the best one?" I called out. We'd only been out for a few hours and had many more ahead of us; it seemed a little disappointing to have already seen the best.

"Yes." The guide struggled to be heard over the roar of the water. "The very best."

My husband touched my face and said something I

couldn't understand—I couldn't hear anything then except for the magnificent thunder of the falls—but I looked at him like I did. The guide produced a camera, and my husband put his arm around me. He had the guide take photos from every angle imaginable; it went on for so long, smiling became painful. The whole time, my husband kept talking to me. I watched his lips move, but I missed every word.

That night, back at Las Grutas, we made love in the shower, the water turned off, his hand wrapped around the back of my neck. Near the end, he accidentally brushed against my nose and I cried out in pain. Afterward, we lay in bed for a long time without speaking; I would have liked to believe it was the blissful quiet that can follow a spectacular day, but it felt like a different kind of silence.

Eventually he fell asleep. I stayed awake. I tried counting backward from five hundred. I tried watching shadows twitch on the ceiling. I tried picturing us standing on that bridge, the Garganta del Diablo cascading behind us, but all I could see was a great wall of water, blindingly white and falling like an avalanche.

I got out of bed, dressed, and slipped out of our room. In the lobby, the manager's office door was locked, the front desk unattended. I left the hotel and walked down to the beach, thinking about what my husband might have said to me on that bridge. I assumed he was saying beautiful things—how he felt about us, our life together—but maybe I was wrong. Maybe my doubt was infectious. Maybe he was no longer sure what his capacities were. The water was dark and rolling. Something prickly brushed against my ankle. I sat on a rock and faced the ocean. I rested my hands over my nose, as I had on the plane, and listened to the hushed sound of my breath.

The beach was so dark that if the moon hadn't shifted and cast a fan of light onto the strip of water I happened to be watching, I might have missed her altogether. But when the profile of a swimming woman entered my field of vision, I recognized Christina Humbolt from the way her hair was gathered at the nape, just as it had been at the cocktail reception, and the slim shape of her shoulders. I imagined her husband sleeping soundly in their room, unaware that his wife had slipped into a dimension of her own. Or, for all I knew, she went swimming every night and told her husband about it the next morning over breakfast. Other people's lives were no less impossible to understand than my own.

She stopped swimming and looked toward the beach. I waved, first casually and then more vigorously, crisscrossing my arms over my head like I was in need of rescue. I wanted her to come to land. I wanted to ask her things about the life she led. But she just looked in my direction for a long time, her body bobbing in the water, before continuing. She had seen me, I was certain, but she wasn't coming out to meet me.

I moved my tongue across my teeth, pushing upward until the pressure translated into a bright line of pain. Soon I lost sight of Christina, but I didn't want to go back to my room. Instead I raked the sand with my fingers and thought about how for as long as I could remember, I'd felt an emptiness where other things were supposed to be.

I opened my mouth and started packing it with fistfuls of damp sand. The grains scratched the roof of my mouth and got wedged between my teeth. Grit ran down the back of my throat. My cheeks ballooned; sand stuck to my gums. It became difficult to breathe. I imagined my body filling up like an hourglass; I imagined my husband or the hotel manager or Christina Humbolt finding me on this rock the next morning, weighted down like a carnival dummy. I kept going until I could barely breathe, until I couldn't close my mouth, until I was leaking sand. And then I coughed it all out, my shoulders heaving as wet clumps fell to the ground.

Days later, I would still be finding the evidence, a grain stuck in a molar, a scratch on my tongue. One afternoon, at lunch, I would blow my nose and notice specks of sand on the tissue. And years later, after Patagonia was far behind us, this was the moment I would remember—because I had acted inexplicably in the middle of the night and I never had to explain myself.

———

The second thing to go wrong was finding out that my husband had broken my nose. Three days after our trip to Iguazú, I woke to an unbearable cluster of pain in the bridge. My husband was already awake. He was standing at the bathroom mirror and shaving, a white towel wrapped around his waist. I rose and went into the bathroom.

"My god," he said when he saw me, his face half-full of lather. "The swelling is much worse."

I looked in the mirror. My nose resembled one of the fat black dates we'd been served at breakfast. I felt something wet coming down my face and held out my palm; I watched as tiny drops of blood dotted my skin.

"I feel dizzy," I said to my husband, then leaned over and threw up in the toilet. He put down his razor and called the front desk. After he hung up, he helped me back into bed.

"They're sending a doctor," he said before returning to the bathroom to finish shaving. From the bed, I could see his arm moving up and down, graceful and controlled. The last three days had been a continuous circuit of morning walks on the beach and afternoon excursions to San Antonio Oeste and cocktail hours in the lobby. The routine had become so familiar, the details of our life in Philadelphia had started to seem vague and remote, as though that existence had never really been ours at all.

The doctor was a tall, hollow-cheeked man with smoke-colored eyebrows. He wore a khaki suit with a red flower stuck in the lapel and carried a black briefcase.

"Are you the patient?" he asked.

"Yes," my husband answered for me. He sat at the foot of the bed, dressed and freshly shaved.

The doctor pulled a chair to the bed and asked me to sit up. He pressed the outside of my nose and I gasped. He opened his briefcase and took out an instrument that looked like pliers with a little metal cone attached to the top. He asked me to tilt my head back.

He slipped the cone inside one of my nostrils and I felt the skin stretch. He took out a miniature flashlight and shone it upward. He squinted and muttered and moved the instrument around. My eyes watered and I could see only my husband in my periphery, a faceless blur on the edge of the bed.

The doctor removed the instrument and turned off the flashlight. "It's broken," he said, patting my blanketed knee.

"What do we do?" my husband asked. He was standing now, hovering over the doctor and his black case.

"It will heal on its own," the doctor said. He suggested ice packs and time. "But this will help with the pain." He took out a prescription bottle, tapped a dozen white pills into his palm, and left them on the bedside table.

He gathered his instruments and washed his hands in the bathroom. My husband brought me a glass of water. The first painkiller was sluggish going down and the aftertaste was that of sand.

"How did this happen again?" the doctor asked, his hand on the door.

"An emergency landing," my husband said. His tone was suddenly sharp. "There was turbulence. It was an accident."

"Our plane was on the news," I added, already drowsy. When the doctor left, it felt like the end of a dream.

"Can you believe he suspected me?" my husband asked when the doctor was gone. He paced in front of the bed. "That's just insulting."

The room had become tilted and blurry. He appeared to be standing on a slope and our white ceiling looked like it was made of light. I found a grain of sand hidden beneath my tongue and swallowed it.

"It was an accident," I said before falling asleep.


A sketch of the suspect: after getting married, I visited my parents only on holidays. Once I saw an X-ray of a heart and I was alarmed by its smallness, its translucence. A thing we ask entirely too much of. On our way to Patagonia I'd watched the planes in holding patterns at the Buenos Aires airport and thought about how that used to be me. I had landed somewhere, finally, even if I couldn't point it out on a map. After I had been married for a year, I dreamed about my dead sister. In the dream she was a child, maybe six or seven. She didn't look anything like me. She had dark shiny hair and was jumping rope on a playground. When she saw me, she put down the rope and said, "What the fuck are you doing?" And I said, "This is all your fault." I was married for three years before I told my husband I wasn't an only child, like him, and that was just because my mother brought my sister up at Thanksgiving. Once I took a long lunch and went to see a tarot card reader on Tasker Street. It was my first week back from Patagonia and whenever I was stopped at a red light, I had fantasies of simply getting out of the car and walking away, leaving the keys in the ignition, the radio on. When the tarot reader drew the Hanged Man, she said that meant I should do the opposite of what I would normally do. Which was fine advice if you understand what it is that you do.

I had two more pills before going to the cocktail reception in the lobby, where I drank three medio medios and stood swaying next to my husband as a new couple introduced themselves. They were the Meyer-Stewards and they too were on their honeymoon.

"Married just a week," Susannah Meyer-Steward said, a martini in one hand and a king crab leg in the other.

"I can't believe we're in Patagonia," Patrick Meyer-Steward said. He was bald except for a thin halo of hair on the back of his head, and drinking scotch on the rocks. "I wanted to go to France."

"How did you meet?" my husband asked them.

"On a cruise in the Bahamas," Patrick said. "Last July."

"It was kind of a singles thing, but of course I didn't really expect to meet anyone," Susannah said. "Then one afternoon I saw Patrick, playing shuffleboard on the deck."

"Shuffleboard!" I called out, louder than I should have. "How charming."

"We had a shuffleboard game at our wedding," Patrick said. "It was island-themed. All the bridesmaids wore leis."

"The newly initiated really do tell the best stories." I placed my empty glass on the tray of a passing waiter. Across the room, I saw Christina Humbolt standing next to her husband. I could almost hear her making polite party chatter in her easy British way.

"Aren't you on your honeymoon too?" Susannah asked, her round face crinkling with confusion or the beginnings of worry.

"Yes," I said. "I suppose we are." I felt as though I were hovering just above the ground. I hooked myself around my husband's elbow. "But doesn't it feel like it's been ages?" I said. "Ages and ages and ages?"

He pulled away from me and learned toward the Meyer-Stewards. "She broke her nose," he whispered. "During the emergency landing."

Patrick sipped his drink; Susannah sucked on her crab leg.

"You broke it," I said, tapping my cheekbone. "My husband broke my nose."

"What was that?" Patrick asked, rattling the ice around in his glass.

"My husband broke my nose." I felt like signing those words to the entire room. "He broke it with his elbow."

"She doesn't know what she's talking about," my husband said. "It was an accident."

The Meyer-Stewards excused themselves to see when dinner would be served. I watched them walk away, Susannah still holding the king crab leg, until they disappeared behind a white marble column.

"You're drunk," my husband said, and I suppose that was true, although it didn't feel that way at the time. I simply knew that I should not tell the Meyer-Stewards about the waterfalls and the beaches and the six endemic species of birds and the medio medios. I should show them the truth because the truth was meant to be seen, not just released in the middle of the night.

"Let's go to the room." He stroked the back of my head. I recognized it was happening, but I couldn't connect with the feeling of his fingers in my hair. "We'll order up some food."

"For the first time I feel conscious," I said.

"Jesus Christ," he said. "What did that doctor give you?"

I shrugged myself free and wandered toward the bathroom. He let me go. I went over to the staircase that led to the dining room and walked up and down the steps for a while, then drifted back toward the lobby. I passed the manager's office; the door was open, the TV on. I leaned against the doorway and moved my tongue over my gums. It took me a minute to realize that the office wasn't empty this time. Someone was sitting in the manager's chair, her back to the door.

"Hola," I said.

The chair spun around, and there was Christina Humbolt, her legs crossed, a drink in her hand.

I stepped into the office, and right away, I looked for proof of her swimming—a strand of wet hair, the faint scent of seawater—but found nothing.

"Have a sip of this." She held out her glass. "It's a medio medio times two."

I took her drink. The glass was cold and damp and soon my hand went numb.

"I'm finally conscious," I said to Christina.

"So you are." She slouched in the chair, her crisp accent dulled. The guanaco scarf hung limply from her neck and she had taken her hair down; the ends, slightly curled, rested on her shoulders.

"And I keep finding sand everywhere," I told her. "It's in my mouth. Is it in your mouth too?"

She sighed. "What do you want me to say?"

"Something definitive," I said. "Something useful."

She took back the glass and drank. "Your husband seems to think you're not feeling well."

"He sent you after me?"

"He thinks he did."

"How did you know where I'd be?"

"Lucky guess," she said, handing me the glass. "It's quiet in here."

"I'm feeling fine," I said. "Much better, actually."

"Don't expect it to last."

I finished the drink. She aimed a remote at the TV and turned up the volume.

"What's on?" I asked.

"Nothing good," she said. "The news."

We gazed up at the TV and watched bulldozers and backhoes crowd around an excavation of some sort. Or perhaps the construction of a new building was beginning. A reporter stood in front of the site with a microphone. She was a woman, and the wind blew her hair across her face. The words "dirt" and "night" were all I could understand. On the plane to Brazil, my husband found a *National Geographic* in his seat pocket and showed me a photo spread of the Karajá, an indigenous group living in the Brazilian Amazon. The photos were from an initiation ceremony. The boys' faces were painted with black; dark circles had been smudged beneath their eyes. I remembered thinking that they weren't their real selves anymore, that the self had been forsaken in order to be part of something larger, a lesson I'd tried to teach myself but never really learned.

"Excavación," the reporter said, which I understood to

mean "digging." *Are they digging the sand out of us?* I wanted to ask Christina.

"Excavación, excavación," the reporter said again.


The third thing to go wrong was the hotel catching fire. We were awoken by an alarm at three in the morning and when we stepped into the hallway, hotel employees, one of whom I recognized as the manager, were herding guests from their rooms. There was a fire on the top floor of the hotel, the manager said when he came upon us, his maroon uniform stained with sweat. A penthouse guest left a cigar burning. We were instructed to take the stairs down to the courtyard outside. Bottled water and blankets would be provided. The manager told us not to worry.

The stairs were flooded with guests. I grabbed my husband's elbow and he put his hand over mine. Earlier that night I never went back to the cocktail party. I'd left Christina Humbolt alone in the manager's office, gone upstairs, taken another pill, and fallen asleep fully clothed on top of the bed. I didn't know what time my husband came back to the room, only that he didn't bother waking me, so I was one of the only guests not wearing pajamas or slippers or bathrobes.

"I hope we don't die," I said.

"Don't be absurd," my husband replied, squeezing my fingers.

Outside we congregated a safe distance from the hotel, the sea cliffs behind us, a black ridge in the darkness. We watched smoke collect above the resort. It hovered over the building the way smog hangs over a factory. The air thickened and warmed.

By then the drugs had worn off and my nose was killing me. *This will never stop*, I thought, pressing a fist against my forehead. But within two weeks the pain and the swelling would be gone, the bruising reduced to a yellow spot or two, though my face would never look quite the same. There would always be a slight crook in my nose, only visible if you examined me head-on. Over time, I would come to believe my husband and I were the only ones who knew it was there.

We had been watching the fire for a minute or two before there was a cracking noise and bright orange flames burst through one of the top windows. Someone screamed and I was reminded of how, as our airplane tumbled toward the earth, I'd thought of our passports in their black nylon cases and our plastic toiletries bags and the international cell phone we'd rented, everything tucked neatly away in our suitcases, and was stricken by the notion of rescue workers pulling these possessions from the rubble and using them to determine who we were.

"I think we're going to have to take another honeymoon," my husband said. "This can't be what we think of when we remember our honeymoon. It just can't."

"Should we take this as a sign?" I said. "That this whole time we've been trailed by disaster?"

"It's a coincidence," my husband said. "There's no such thing as signs."

I watched fire balloon out of the building.

The guests had scattered, some of them standing near the edge of the sea cliffs and facing the water. I heard sirens, but they sounded too far away to believe they would arrive in time to do much good.

My husband tugged on my sleeve. He was pointing at a group of four that were huddled together. It was the Humbolts and the Meyer-Stewards, all of them in hotel-issued white bathrobes and slippers. "We should be standing with them," he said.

When he started toward them, I hung back. I was watching Christina Humbolt, who kept untying and retying her sash. Had she been out swimming? Or already returned to her room and, when the alarms woke her husband, pretended she'd been beside him all along? Her face was luminous with sweat; from a distance, her hair appeared darker and sleeker, like it might be damp.

When my husband reached the Humbolts and the Meyer-Stewards, he turned and looked for me, but other people had spilled into the path between us. He waved his hand above his head and called my name, but still I did not go to him. I heard the sirens again, louder now, and the hotel manager had started handing out little fleece blankets

and bottled water, just as he had promised. The space between my husband and me grew more congested—*I looked
for you*, he would say when we were finally reunited—and
soon I wasn't able to see him at all.

A boom sounded, loud as the rushing of the Garganta
del Diablo. Fire spilled from the hotel like an outstretched
hand. Right then I longed to go back inside, to our room
that overlooked the sea. To sift through our wallets and the
backpacks we carried on day trips, to lay the contents out
on the bed like evidence and try to understand what it was
that was going to be lost.

OPA-LOCKA

My sister was the photographer. From a rooftop deck, nestled between two enormous ferns in clay pots, she photographed our target, Mr. Defonte, entering the adjacent apartment building. He wore a white linen suit, boat shoes, and a straw sun hat with a chin strap that dangled beneath his jaw.

"Only in Florida," Julia said, snapping a photo. "Does he think he's on a safari?"

Mr. Defonte paused outside and stared at his feet. He was only a few steps away from the entrance of the glossy high-rise building. The doors were made of blue glass with silver handles in the shape of leaping fish. Julia took another picture. I was crouched beside my sister and peering through binoculars. I could see his face in profile, his long downward-sloping nose and soft chin. I knew his full legal name, his social, his date of birth, where he lived, where he worked, his favorite lunch spot, and his license plate number. His wife had hired me and Julia to investigate him. Together we made up Winslow & Co., the private detective firm we'd been running for the last year.

"I don't think he's going inside." I lowered the binoculars. It was Boca Raton in June. My throat was slick with sweat, my underarms damp. "I just have a feeling."

"If that motherfucker doesn't walk through that door, I'm going to climb down from this roof and smack him in the face," Julia said. The apples of her cheeks were flushed. Her chestnut hair glistened.

I opened the red cooler we brought on stakeouts and fished out an ice cube. I ran it along the back of Julia's neck and over her cheeks. She sighed in a way that sounded grateful. I kept moving the ice over her skin until it turned into a tiny translucent shard and melted into my fingertips, until it was just my hand on the nape of her neck.

Mr. Defonte opened the door. He hesitated for a moment, then disappeared into the building. Julia snapped three pictures in a row. Now all he had to do was come out. And all we had to do was wait.

*What do you want?* That was how the conversation with Mrs. Defonte began, how they always began. You don't hire a private investigator unless you want something. In our early twenties, Julia and I hired a detective to track down our father, who vanished in the middle of the night when we were teenagers. I was fifteen, Julia thirteen. We just woke up one Saturday morning and found him gone and our mother in the backyard, staring at the sky. Our detective was expensive and didn't have any luck. We knew what it was like to want something so badly, it burned a hole inside you.

Mrs. Defonte had hired us for the same reason most women hired PIs: she suspected her husband was having an affair. In the last six months, she explained in her living room, his behavior had changed. He took phone calls in the middle of the night. He worked later. Something about his tone of voice was different, his smell, even. He seemed to have trouble looking her in the eye. She had followed him once, waited outside his office and trailed him to a café on Second Street, but then she lost her nerve.

Mrs. Defonte had beautiful black hair that nested on her shoulders and nails painted the color of pink geraniums. She wore a snug black sleeveless dress, a white sweater draped over her shoulders, and sat with her ankles crossed. She was in her fifties, around the same age as my mother, who was several weeks into a six-month cruise around the world; it had started in Fort Lauderdale and would end in Monte Carlo. Julia liked to joke that our mother had been away at sea her whole life. She'd done her best to raise us, but once we were out in the world, the distance that had always been there shifted and hardened, like a building shedding its scaffolding and assuming its final shape. We reminded her of painful times, we understood.

"I want to know what's real," Mrs. Defonte said.

"That's exactly what we do." We had been served iced

teas and Julia's long fingers were wrapped around her glass. "We gather facts, evidence. We separate what's true from what isn't."

Mrs. Defonte nodded. "It's all very peculiar," she said, almost to herself.

"It's actually pretty common," I said. Julia stepped on the toe of my sneaker. I had a habit of saying the wrong thing to clients. All were supposed to think their predicament was special, in need of our expertise. The Defonte case was a big opportunity for us. We'd been getting most of our work from insurance companies, which often hired private investigators to look into claims, but it was the domestic investigations that really paid.

Mrs. Defonte looked at the ceiling for a moment and sighed. She told us that sometimes she wondered if she was making it up. Once she wrote out a list of all the warning signs, all the things he'd done, but on paper it didn't look that damning. Still she couldn't let go of the feeling that something was wrong. It plagued her day and night.

"Maybe I just have too much time on my hands," she said.

"You leave it to us," Julia said. "Give us a month and we'll know what he's been up to."

On our way out, I noticed a photo in a silver frame. It was Mrs. Defonte standing on a stage, a red velvet curtain hanging behind her. She wore a long bronze gown. Her hands were clasped in front her stomach, her lips parted in song.

"I sing in our community opera," Mrs. Defonte said when she saw me looking. "That was from *The Mask of Orpheus*. I went to Juilliard, you know."

"Really?" I glanced up at her. She was nearly smiling.

"It was a long time ago." She opened the front door and watched us walk to our car, a black Explorer with tinted windows and a portable GPS affixed to the dashboard. It was a rental.

That night, back at our apartment, a minimal amount of digging turned up the name of the community opera and its rehearsal schedule. They staged their rehearsals and performances at an opera house in downtown Boca Raton. My sister and I lived in Opa-locka, ten miles north of Miami. Opa-locka came from the Indian name Opatish-awokalocka, which meant "the high land north of the little river on which there is a camping place." It was a rough neighborhood. Every night, Julia locked all our equipment—GPS, walkie-talkies, tape recorders, cameras, binoculars, laptops—in a safe in her bedroom closet. She kept the Glock 22 I was licensed for on the bedside table. Just last week our neighbor Mirabella had been robbed at knifepoint. I had tried to talk my sister into moving, citing crime statistics and reasonable rents in other neighborhoods, but she loved the two-story blue stucco building with the concrete balcony and the drained swimming pool half-filled with bottles and empty cigarette packs. For Julia, risk was like air. The good news was that we saved a bundle in rent and could afford to run ads in everything from the South Florida *Sun-Sentinel* to the *Boca Beacon*, which was how Mrs. Defonte had found us.

One night, a week into the Defonte case, I told Julia I needed to go for a drive. It took less than an hour to reach the opera house. It was on a brick street lined with palm trees, a circular building with a glass facade, so even from the parking lot, I could see the warm light inside. A crescent-shaped pool curved in front of the entrance; a trio of fountainheads shot white water into the air. After finding the rehearsal stage, I took a seat in the very back. The space was empty save for a handful of people in the front rows. They were in rehearsal for *Don Giovanni*. Mrs. Defonte stood on the right-hand side of the stage. She wore street clothes, black slacks and a crisp pink button-down. A long white veil was clipped to her hair. A man with a black mask over his eyes stood in the center of the stage, singing. I watched Mrs. Defonte watch the man and wondered what she was feeling. Another person came into the theater and walked down the aisle, carrying an armful of fake roses to the stage. I sank lower into my seat.

The veil Mrs. Defonte wore in her hair was not unlike the one I'd worn when I got married. I had moved in with Julia six months ago, after my divorce was finalized, and soon I'd started getting strange postcards in the mail. They were part of a set. I'd seen a similar kind of thing in a party store once; if I had all the cards they would fit together like a puzzle. So far, I'd received two swatches of sky, a cloud, a dried-out river, and a brown ledge. There was nothing on the back except my name and Julia's address. Everything was typed, the letters large and a little smudged, as though it had been done on an old typewriter. The postmarks were from Arizona, Utah, Nevada. I had never seen my husband use a typewriter, but he had always wanted to travel west. He thought Florida was a miserable swamp. And he knew Julia's would be the first place I'd turn. Once, I spread the cards out on the floor and tried to put them in order. I didn't have enough pieces to make sense of what they were supposed to be.

When Mrs. Defonte began singing, my hands dropped into my lap. My chin rose, as though pulled by a string. Each note was as perfect as the crystal goblets I'd noticed on her dining room table. The other actors on stage gazed at her with the same kind of wonder. When she finished, they all applauded. One person rose from her seat. Mrs. Defonte looked around, startled, like she'd just come out of a trance. A voice like that was a weapon.

By ten o'clock, we'd been on the roof for seven hours. The darkness had brought little relief from the heat. We'd used up all the ice cubes, eaten the bologna sandwiches I'd packed, drunk a beer apiece. Over the last two weeks, we had observed Mr. Defonte entering hotels, high-end places near his office, and exiting after an hour; it was always the same days of the week, the same times. Fifteen minutes after he left, the same blond woman always emerged. From the blonde's photo and license plate number, we located her address and tracked Mr. Defonte to her high-rise on Royal Palm Avenue. The first time we followed him to her building, it was observational; this time, we were prepared to document. Catching him going in and out of her residence was significant to our case. The hotel meetings could, with some effort, be explained away. He was a lawyer, after all. He could say he was meeting clients, that the blonde's presence was a coincidence. Spending seven-plus hours in her building, however, would be harder to dismiss.

When it was my turn to watch the door, Julia stretched out on one of the white plastic beach chairs behind me. The chairs had mildew on them, which we hoped meant the roof deck didn't get much use. If anyone discovered us, Julia planned to tell them we were police. Before starting Winslow & Co., we enrolled in an online detective school. We learned how to take fingerprints and write reports, how to run credit and background checks, how to do surveillance and skip tracing. I liked the school; it made everything seem official. At the end, there was a certificate. Julia was less interested, so I did most of the work for our classes. One thing we were never supposed to do was impersonate a police officer.

Around midnight, the conversation turned to our father.

"Here's a story," I said to Julia.

Once, my father told me a story about a business trip to

Chicago with his friend Bill Keller. At a bar, Bill picked up two prostitutes. They were young, with accents and fake fur coats. They all went back to a hotel, an old grand place called the Iron Horse. My father and Bill disappeared into separate rooms, but instead of doing what one would normally do with a prostitute, of doing what Bill Keller was doing in that very same moment, my father said they lay down on his bed and he read to her.

"Read what?" I'd asked.

"A novel," my father had said.

I was eleven. The story made me feel strange. It seemed to come out of nowhere. We were eating lunch at Bojangles'. The Kingsmen were playing on the radio. I knew what a prostitute was, but I didn't yet understand how unusual it was to not do what one normally does with a prostitute, to read her a novel instead. I didn't understand that my father wanted me to see him as being above temptation and superior to Bill Keller, who I had never met. I didn't know the right questions to ask. *What kind of novel? What did she smell like? Did she fall asleep on your arm? What was her name?* Now I thought I would like to find that prostitute and get her side of the story.

"So?" Julia said, her voice drowsy from the heat.

"I realized the other day that it couldn't possibly be true. I don't think I ever saw Dad read anything, let alone novels, for starters."

"What *was* true?" Julia said.

Our father was a grifter. He spent our childhood selling fake insurance policies. When he vanished, he left
behind a mountain of debt; the house we'd grown up in
went to the bank. Our mother moved us to Athens,
Georgia, where she was from. She threw away all the photos we had of our father and encouraged us to tell people
he was dead. All we were left with was the stories. The
prostitute in Chicago. The time he escaped the Vietcong by
jumping off a cliff. The time he ran with the bulls in Bar-
celona and saved his best friend from being gored in the
ass. Things only children would believe. All story and no
truth.

I liked to tell myself that, unlike our father, we were on
the right side of the law, me and Julia, with our firm and
its solid-sounding name, but that hadn't always been the
case. Two years ago, Julia was arrested for breaking into
houses. She'd been at it for a long time, picking places
where the owners were away. When she finally got caught,
in a mansion on Fisher Island, she did six months in Brow-
ard Correctional. The idea for the private detective business was hatched during visitation. We talked about how
exciting it would be, how lucrative. My husband, a tax
consultant for H&R Block, had always thought Julia was
a professional housesitter; he was furious that I had lied to
him, that I'd once gone down to Coral Gables to swim in
the Olympic-size pool of an estate my sister was robbing,
and even more furious that I insisted on visiting her twice

a week in jail. *Can't you just write to her?* he'd say. *Do you have to actually go there?* Our mother talked about Julia like she was away on a long trip. So it was just my sister and me, like always.

In Georgia, we had gotten bored with college and dropped out, drifting back to South Florida like homing pigeons. I met my husband while working at a watch store in Pinecrest. He brought a Swiss Army in for repair. He'd had it for a decade; he said he liked to hold on to things. We married a year later, in the Miami courthouse. I loved him, but I didn't always understand how to be honest. Over time, we became less sure we were something the other wanted to hold on to. And then there was Julia's arrest and visitation. I saw how small she looked in her gray jumpsuit, how she wanted to ask if our mother was coming but knew better. As I listened to her talk about the PI business—her voice quick and grasping—I realized my thirties were on the horizon and I'd never had a job I found interesting. And that I liked the idea of busting people for doing things they shouldn't be. Since Julia had a record, I'd been the one to apply for our firearm and PI licenses. I told my husband Julia and I were starting a catering company. When he discovered a Winslow & Co. business card in my purse, he bypassed fury and went straight to sadness.

"Do you think Bill Keller was a real person?" my sister asked.

"I don't know." I pulled at the collar of my T-shirt; the fabric was stuck to my skin. "The hotel is a real place, though. The Iron Horse. I looked it up once."

"Any sign of Defonte?" I could tell she was ready to change the subject.

I raised the binoculars and scanned the entrance. The perimeter of the building was brightly lit and still. "Nothing," I said. We were prepared to keep waiting. There were two more beers, a thermos of water, and a bag of Cheetos in the cooler, plus a packet of NoDoz in the back pocket of my shorts.

"Maybe Mrs. Defonte is out of town," Julia said.

"Maybe." I happened to know that was unlikely, since she'd had rehearsal the night before and had it again tomorrow.

We waited through the night, and when the sun rose behind us, it brought a heat that was painful. We put on big sunglasses and baseball caps and draped towels over our shoulders. I'd taken too many NoDoz and my hands were shaky, my mouth dry. All the water was gone. We had not taken our eyes off the building since he went inside, not for one single moment.

Julia searched around with the binoculars. I rested my elbows on the edge of the roof. It was unusual for a target to change the pattern so rapidly, to go from one-hour stretches to all-nighters. Maybe Mrs. Defonte really was out of town. Or maybe he had decided to up and leave her.

"Keep looking," she said, passing me the binoculars. "I'll go get us coffee."

"Water," I said. "I feel like I'm being roasted."

A lot of PI-ing was about waiting. Knowing how to wait, being prepared to wait, not giving up on waiting even when it felt like God was one of those assholey kids who hold a magnifying glass over ants until they explode, only He's using the sun. What we didn't know was that sometimes all the waiting in the world won't give you what you need.

After twenty-four hours, we decided something had to be done. It felt like we had been on the roof for years. We'd been trading off for bathroom breaks. Julia had made two runs to the convenience store down the street for water, Nutri-Grain bars, and coffee (while she was at it, she had checked to make sure Mr. Defonte's car was still parked in the same spot; it was). Still, we couldn't stay up there forever. My stomach gurgled. The back of my neck and my legs were sunburned. My eyes itched. Birds had shit on our camera bag and on Julia's wrist. Mr. Defonte had to come out of there eventually, we figured. It was a Wednesday. He had a wife, a job. But the blazing afternoon stretched on and on until finally it was night again.

"We should call Mrs. Defonte," Julia said. "See if she's heard from him." She tossed me the cell phone and said she was going out for more coffee. She liked to do the talking until we had to tell clients something they might not want to hear.

I kneeled on the roof, facing the building Mr. Defonte had vanished into. I'd never had a conversation with Mrs. Defonte alone.

"Do you have any news?" she asked when I called. I closed my eyes for a moment and imagined what her words would sound like if she were singing them.

"Sort of," I said. "Have you heard from your husband lately?"

She said that she hadn't. He was on a business trip in Memphis.

"That can't be true. We photographed him going into an apartment building on Royal Palm yesterday afternoon."

"And?"

"We haven't seen him since," I said. "We've been watching the building. He hasn't come out yet."

She was silent. I guessed she was considering what her husband had been doing in that building for so long and who he'd been doing it with. I pictured her sitting stiffly on the elegant sofa with the cream-colored cushions and the curved wood legs, a hand resting on her knee.

Mrs. Defonte said she would call me back and did so a few minutes after we hung up. She reported that she had tried her husband's cell, twice, but there was no answer. When my husband left, I had wanted to call him very badly, but had gotten drunk instead; at the time I told myself I was washing the urge out of me. I wondered if another postcard had turned up at Julia's apartment in Opa-locka.

"I guess we're not sure what to do," I said, worried Mrs. Defonte might start losing faith in us. "We've been up here a long time."

"You're the detectives," she said.

When morning came, Julia sucked down a coffee and two jelly doughnuts. She picked up the black nylon messenger bag that contained the Defonte case file, stalked over to the fire escape, and started climbing down.

"Where are you going?" I said. "You just made a breakfast run."

"Fuck this motherfucker," Julia said, her hands gripping the ladder.

I followed her down the fire escape. She didn't check for cars before crossing the street. When I caught up with her, she was looking for the blond woman's name on the row of silver mailboxes in the lobby.

"There she is." Julia pointed at box 703. Belinda Singer. Flecks of icing were stuck to her finger.

"This isn't what we do," I said. Private investigators were watchers, waiters. We waited for people to do whatever it was they were going to do, recorded it, and then handed over the evidence. We didn't jump into the middle of situations. We didn't intervene.

"We went to detective school, am I right?"

"*I* went to detective school," I said. "I did all the work. Everything is in my name."

"Well, we call ourselves detectives, don't we?"

I gave her a little shrug. The lack of sleep had made everything bleary.

"I'm ready to do some detecting." Julia held me in a hard stare. She had bright hazel eyes, more green than brown, and could be very convincing.

We rode the elevator to the seventh floor and knocked on the blond woman's door. She looked older up close, her tanned skin creased lightly around the eyes and forehead, her lips thin and dry. She wore a white sleeveless tennis dress and white sneakers with ankle socks. Her hair was pulled into a high ponytail.

"Are you Belinda Singer?" Julia flipped open her wallet and flashed the heavy brass badge issued to licensed PIs; if you didn't look closely, it could pass for the real thing. "Let us in. We're detectives. Police."

The woman didn't move from the doorway. I peered over her shoulder, but didn't see anyone inside.

"Ms. Singer? Did you hear me?" My sister's voice was forceful. I would have believed anything she said. The blond woman opened the door a little wider. Julia edged into the apartment.

"You're a detective too?" she asked as I entered.

I glared at her in a way I hoped was intimidating.

My sister moved into the blond woman's living room. She stood on a leopard-print rug, next to a glass coffee table piled high with issues of *South Florida Living*. I hung out closer to the front door. The floor was cream tile; large cockleshells, each the color of a sunset, had been arranged on the pale pink walls.

"Where is Peter Defonte?" Julia asked.

The woman cocked her head. "Who is Peter Defonte?"

Julia told the woman that she knew exactly who Peter Defonte was, that he had been in this apartment for the last two nights and was probably still here.

"I wish," the blond woman said.

"Do you think this is a joke, Ms. Singer?" Julia replied.

"No one's been here. Look around."

We checked the two bedrooms, the closets, the bathrooms. We looked under the beds and behind the shower curtains. When we were finished, Julia pulled a head shot of Mr. Defonte from her messenger bag and handed it to the blond woman.

"This man, we know that you know him." Julia's voice was softer. She touched the woman's forearm. "Go on, take a look."

The woman pinched the sides of the photo and frowned. "I don't know him at all." She handed the photo back to Julia and surveyed us for a moment, her nose wrinkling like she'd just smelled something unpleasant, which was entirely possible, seeing as we'd been baking on the roof, unshowered, for two days.

"I think your detecting skills need some work," she told us.

"This is the law you're talking to," Julia said. And then we got out of the apartment as quickly as we could. We went back down to the ground floor and showed the photo to the building manager, the superintendent, and a few maintenance men. If anyone asked, Julia did the badge flash and said we were police. No one recognized Mr. Defonte. The maintenance men showed us the side entrance, which had been visible from the roof. Besides the front door, that was the only way out; there was nothing that went through the back.

"Not unless you're Spider-Man," one of the men said, moving a mop across the floor.

In our time with Mr. Defonte, he had never seemed wily or agile, like some kind of escape artist. To me he had always looked weak, with his sluggish gait and doughy face and ridiculous hat. Outside I sat on the sidewalk and slumped against the building. The heat was as strong as ever. I felt like my skin was melting.

"What the fucking fuck?" Julia paced in front of me.

I pressed my face against my knees and groaned.

Later we had to call Mrs. Defonte and tell her we'd lost her husband. She'd phoned his office in Boca Raton and the firm he was supposed to be meeting in Memphis; no one had seen or heard from him. He had simply vanished. Since it had been forty-eight hours, Mrs. Defonte called 911 and then the real police got involved.

We had *seen* him go into that building. We had *seen* him open the door and walk inside. Our stakeout had just started; we were sharp and rested and hydrated. We had taken photos. Could he have slipped out when we were on the seventh floor, even though no one saw anything? Can buildings eat people? At a certain point that seemed as likely as anything.

We were required to turn our camera and film over to the police. They had examined every inch of the building, impounded his car and searched it for clues, and were as flummoxed as we were. Me and Julia and Mrs. Defonte met with an officer at the Boca Raton police station, a Detective Gregerson. He was an older man dressed in black slacks, sweat-stained shirtsleeves, and orthopedic shoes. He didn't look capable of much, but then neither had Mr. Defonte. He slid the photos we had taken across the metal table and asked Mrs. Defonte if she could identify her husband. She gazed at the photos of him standing on the sidewalk, staring at his feet; reaching for the door; pulling it open and stepping inside. She wore a quarter-sleeve dress patterned with red and pink flowers and leather sandals. Her black hair was pulled into a tight bun. She looked tired and confused, as though she'd just woken up in a place she didn't recognize.

"It's him," she said.

"Are you certain?" Detective Gregerson said.

She nodded and pushed the pictures away.

"What about the blond woman?" I asked.

"Belinda Singer." Julia cracked her knuckles, her go-to move when she was nervous.

"We questioned her," Detective Gregerson said. "She doesn't know anything."

"What about all those pictures of her and Mr. Defonte?"

"Did you ever see them talk to each other? Hold hands?"

"No," Julia and I said.

"Did you ever see them interact in any way? Any contact at all?"

We glanced at each other.

"No," Julia answered for us.

"There you go." He swept his hand to the side, like he'd solved something.

"There you go *what*?" I said. "It's an excessive amount of coincidences."

He sighed. "Fucking PIs."

"What did we do?" Julia slapped her hand against the table.

Detective Gregerson said that, in his experience, if you wanted to go looking for trouble, all you had to do was spend ten minutes with a few PIs.

"It's your aura," he said.

"We never stopped watching that building," I said. We hadn't. Not for a minute, save for when we searched for him inside. That was the one thing I was sure of.

Mrs. Defonte looked at us and then at Detective Gregerson. "I never should have hired them," she said. "I just wanted some answers."

"Don't we all," said the detective.

I didn't think it was fair for Mrs. Defonte to blame us, but at the same time I did feel partly responsible for whatever it was that had happened to her husband, as though our mere presence had set something in motion that might have remained dormant otherwise.

"We tried our best," I said. "We did just what you asked. We were very professional."

"You should have seen the mess they left on the roof," Detective Gregerson said. "Beer cans, food wrappers. Styrofoam cups, which are hell on the environment. And you shouldn't take those caffeine pills." He patted his chest. "Bad for the heart."

Mrs. Defonte folded her hands on the table and sniffed.

When the police found out we'd posed as real detectives, we were charged with impersonating an officer, fined one thousand dollars, and stripped of our private investigator and gun licenses. Winslow & Co. was over. Because Julia had a prior, her probation was extended by five years. The police said that if it weren't for overcrowding, she'd have gone right back to jail. That same week, a man was stabbed to death in the parking lot of our building in Opa-locka. Even after the body was taken away, streaks of dried blood stayed on the asphalt until it rained.

The rest of the Defonte saga unfolded on local TV. *Boca Raton resident vanishes into thin air!* The story got a lot of air time on Florida stations, but never went national. Still, I developed an addiction to the news. I would stay inside for days, reading and watching everything I could find. I would sleep for hours and wake up tired. Some nights I lay on the sofa and thought as hard as I could about what we'd seen, what it meant. Was his body in that building? Was Belinda Singer some kind of criminal mastermind? Had he faked his own disappearance and made off to South America? What had we missed? I didn't come to a firm conclusion about anything.

Julia had no patience for my brooding. The Defonte case reminded us all too much of our father—not just the vanishing, but the inscrutability of it. My sister threw away our Winslow & Co. business cards and letterhead and started working with a shady, unlicensed PI outfit, whose clients were usually as culpable as the people they wanted investigated—a husband with domestic violence priors looking for his wife, a crooked businessman searching for the equally crooked partner who fleeced him. I brought this up to Julia one night, the morality of it. *Who isn't guilty*, she said, and maybe she had a point. On the nights she didn't come home at all, I would wait up on the sofa, in the glow of the TV, and worry.

New postcards arrived in the mail, another cloud and a rocky slope with scrubby bushes. I gathered all the cards and took them next door to Mirabella, who read tea leaves for a living. She was twenty-one, single, and rarely home. She took me into her bedroom. Her walls were covered with posters of tea leaves in various formations. She flopped down on her bed, spread the cards out in the shape of a rainbow, and examined them.

"This is not in Florida." Mirabella lay on her stomach. She had acne scars on her cheeks. She picked up the river and fanned herself with the card. "I don't know what else to tell you. It's hard to say more without all the pieces."

"Harder than reading tea leaves?"

Mirabella said she wasn't charging me and so I couldn't expect her best work. Besides, she added, pointing at one of the posters with the card, the leaves always told the whole story.

"Like I knew I was going to get robbed before it happened," she said.

"If you knew, why didn't you do something?"

"What could I do?" she said. "Not go home?"

I looked at the poster. The tea was a soggy, dark swirl,

like wet dirt in the bottom of a white cup. Maybe I just didn't have a knack for seeing things.

Back at the apartment, I called my husband. If he would tell me what he was sending pieces of and why, I was willing to give him the satisfaction of saying he knew working with my sister would only bring trouble. I tried calling three times, but I couldn't get through; his cell phone had been disconnected. For a while I pretended the beep-beep-beep was my husband trying to reach me. I told myself he was using Morse code, which I had learned about in detective school. *Hello*, I said. *I'm listening.*

One afternoon, when Julia was out on a job, two things happened: Another postcard arrived. It looked like part of a gorge, the same shade of brown rock, WISH YOU typed across the back. The second thing would have been easy to miss. I was unwrapping a Hot Pocket in the kitchenette when I heard something on the news about a man in Nevada who had been arrested for defrauding senior citizens. I left the frozen Hot Pocket on the counter and went to the TV. According to the reporter, this man's racket had been going on for two years. He had raked in hundreds of thousands. A Nevada DA said he would be punished to the fullest extent of the law. They showed the man being led up the steps of the courthouse. His hands were cuffed behind his back. A police officer gripped his elbow. He wore a gray trench coat. The wind blew his white hair across his face, revealing a toupee. He was much older, of course, but there he was.

---

"No fucking way," Julia said when I told her what I had discovered. The eleven o'clock news replayed the story and she gasped when she saw him walking up the courthouse steps. I felt relieved that she'd recognized him as immediately as I had. We called the number our mother had left; her boat was docked in the Maldives and she was on an excursion to a fishing village. We told the cruise director to tell our mother it was an emergency.

For a weekend, Julia partook in my addiction to the news. We kept the TV on day and night. The Senate was considering a bill designed to safeguard the personal information of senior citizens, so our father's story was getting national play. We read everything there was to read on the Web. Julia let her cell phone ring. When we came across more photos online of our father entering the courthouse, she held on to my arm. In one, he was looking right at the camera, his gray eyebrows raised, his lips parted. Age spots dotted his face; his skin sagged. We made fun of his toupee to keep from crying.

The facts went like this: our father, posing as a financial consultant, had convinced seventeen elderly Nevadans to give him power of attorney over their finances and then fraudulently cashed checks on the accounts. The victims had lost everything. It was Mrs. Calhoun, a ninety-six-year-old widow, who got him caught. Her daughter got suspicious of our father and called the authorities. An investigation was launched. When our father was arrested, he was getting ready to skip town. I wondered what, if anything, he would have been leaving behind.

On the first night, we printed news articles and cut out the photos of our father. We sat next to each other on the sofa, the TV blaring, and studied them under a magnifying glass. He and Julia shared the same high forehead and sharp cheekbones. I wondered if there was anything of him she saw in me.

"He looks so old," Julia said, rubbing her thumb over the paper.

When we called our mother a second time, the cruise director was able to get her on the phone. We put Julia's cell on speaker and told our mother everything. That we'd found our father in Nevada. That what had happened to him, where he'd been, was no longer a mystery. We were breathless, talking over each other. Once we finished, we leaned toward the phone and waited.

"We're going to Sri Lanka next," our mother said. "We're going to ride elephants."

"Mom?" we said. "Did you hear what we just told you?"

"This wasn't an emergency," she whispered before hanging up.

On the second night, we watched a TV special called "Preying on the Elderly" that featured our father and a con man right here in Florida, who had defrauded a whole retirement home full of seniors last winter. They showed one of our father's victims, a hunched old man named Reginald. He was leaning into a walker, a tiny white dog at his feet. The program offered a list of tips for elders: Don't give out personal information over the phone. Be suspicious if someone says you've won a fabulous prize. Get-rich-quick schemes never make you rich. Do background checks on everyone you meet. Julia pointed out that it sounded like the elderly were in need of private detectives. I nodded. I hoped Reginald was watching the same thing we were.

Later, while Julia was in the shower, I realized that after our father was arrested, the postcards had stopped coming. I decided they hadn't been from my husband at all, and was surprised by my disappointment. I didn't say anything to my sister at first. I stood by the closed bathroom door and listened to the water. I took a beer from the fridge and drank it standing up. When Julia emerged from the shower, I suggested we watch a movie. I picked up the remote and started clicking through the channels. *Beverly Hills Cop* was on. All night, I kept my secret.

On the third night, I couldn't stop myself from telling Julia about my theory. My husband hadn't sent the cards. It had been our father all along.

"It makes sense," I said. "A bunch were postmarked in Nevada."

"I should have known." Julia was on the couch in a long T-shirt and socks. "A typewriter didn't seem like your husband's style. Too romantic."

I sat next to her. The news was on. Julia turned down the volume. The cards were stacked on the coffee table. He knew where we lived. He had kept track of us. Was it out of love, or a calculation, keeping tabs on his family in case he ran out of strangers to con? More questions we couldn't answer. I wondered if he knew about my divorce and Julia's stint in jail, if he had seen Mr. Defonte on the news and knew it had to do with us.

"I think this one goes here." Julia picked up the image of the gorge and placed it in the middle of the table. We put the sky and the clouds above it. The river to the left, the ledge to the right. We played with the positioning of the cards, tried to complete the sentence that began with WISH YOU.

"Wish you well?" I said.

"Wish you luck?"

"Wish you were here?"

Julia looked at me. "If that's what it says, I'm glad we're not."

In the end, the puzzle didn't tell us much. We still didn't have enough pieces to know what it was for sure. We could tell it was a big dusty valley of some kind. Someplace out west, we figured. That part of the country was foreign to us.

"The Grand Canyon?" I suggested.

"Is it rocky enough?" Julia leaned over the coffee table, her head tilted. "What about Death Valley? That's in Nevada, right?"

I remembered hearing about the salt flats in Death Valley on TV. Badwater, they were called. The only animal that could survive there was some kind of snail. "Or the Mojave, in California? Do deserts have riverbeds?"

Julia scooped up the cards and stacked them on the table.

Years ago, when we were kids, we often played in the woods behind our childhood home. Somehow these nights had the same feeling as our games. At a certain point, Julia would always drop whatever we were doing and bolt into the woods. I would chase her, call after her, but she would just run and run. Finally I would climb the oak in our backyard and search for the peak of her head moving through the trees. I hardly ever found her. Usually I had to wait until she was ready to come out. Sometimes that took minutes; other times, hours.

My sister stared at the TV. I heard sirens. At first it sounded like they were right outside, but after a while, they began to fade.

"Here's a story," she said. "About two little girls who tried to make something out of nothing."


By Monday, Julia had reached her limit. That night she muted the TV and lay on the couch, her head in my lap. I nestled my fingers in her hair. It was thick and tangled and smelled like her coconut shampoo.

"I can't stay in this place anymore," she said.

At first I thought she was talking about Opa-locka and felt a wash of relief. "It's about time. Where do you want to go?"

Julia didn't seem to hear me. "Mom was right. From now on, we should just pretend he's dead."

I pulled my fingers out of her hair. "How can we pretend that? He's right there on the news."

"It's like being in a maze," she said. "We're never going to get anywhere."

She was right. Between Mr. Defonte and our father, I could feel myself being consumed by mystery. But that was beside the point. It didn't even feel like a choice, to wade into all of this. I didn't understand how she could decide to stop.

"I have to let it go." She sat up and rubbed her forehead. "I just have to."

A still of our father was on TV. It was from when he had just arrived in Nevada. He wore a yellow polo shirt and was smiling broadly, a neat crest of gray hair arcing over his forehead. It might have been under the worst circumstances possible, but he was back in our lives.

"Look at him, Julia." I leaned toward her and pressed my palm against her cheek. "He's right there."

"I know he is," she said. "And I wish he wasn't."

After that night, she went back to working with the shady private investigators. She started coming home smelling like whiskey and smoke, a gun tucked into the waistband of her jeans, even though we'd lost the firearm license.

*Just in case*, she told me. She got a pager and it buzzed constantly. She lost weight. Her hair thinned. The spaces beneath her eyes hollowed out. She looked the same as she did in jail, weary and sad. Once I heard her screaming at someone in our parking lot. By the time I looked out the window, my sister was alone and sitting on the ground, her face in her hands. I went downstairs and crouched in front of her, stepping in a small pool of gasoline. I placed my hands on her knees. *Julia*, I said. *Look at me.* She sighed and tipped her head back, and for a moment I thought she was going to break out of whatever it was she'd fallen into. But then she jumped to her feet, went upstairs, and locked herself in her room. A few mornings later, I found her asleep on the couch, fully clothed, the gun on the coffee table. Her brown hair fell over her shoulders; her hands were folded under her chin. Her lips were parted in the exact same way our father's had been in the photo we found online; they even had the same long, slender shape. On the couch, Julia was free of the sadness. She looked innocent and sweet and most people would have no idea what she was capable of. But I knew, because she was my sister. I knew she was keeping things from me.

Here was what I kept from Julia: Twice a month, I would go to Boca Raton for Mrs. Defonte's rehearsals. By late July, they were in final preparations for *Don Giovanni*. They had done the last two rehearsals in full costume; the stage held a pair of elaborate gold balconies connected by a wide staircase. The steps were covered by a plush red rug. A chandelier hung from the ceiling. It was like seeing the opera on opening night, minus the audience. I almost felt bad that I hadn't paid anything.

Mrs. Defonte was playing Donna Anna and the masked man was Don Giovanni. She wore a floor-length gown with lace sleeves and green brocade, the veil still clipped in her black hair. Her voice was as beautiful as ever. I wondered how much she thought about her husband, what she thought about him. I imagined she had theories of her own.

Don Giovanni wore black pants, a white peasant shirt, and a wig. The basic problem in the story was that everyone wanted Don Giovanni to change, but he wouldn't. It also showed how a person's actions come back on him, how the seed of what happens next exists in what's happening now. I had started going to the rehearsals because of Mrs. Defonte, but in the end, Don Giovanni was the one who held my interest.

My favorite scene was set in a graveyard. Don Giovanni and the servant, Leporello, were surrounded by gravestones. Giovanni's laugh summoned the ghost of the Commendatore, who he'd killed in act one. Leporello was frightened; Giovanni invited the Commendatore to dinner. He couldn't know, couldn't see, what would happen next.

It was a terrible flaw, our inability to see where our lives were leading us. For instance, in the back row of the theater, I could never have imagined that in late August, while Julia was stopped at a red light in Opa-locka, three blocks from our apartment, a man would walk up to her and shoot her in the head. She died at the scene. Our mother had to fly back from Muscat, her neck heavy with blue topaz, which, she had been told, would shield her from grief. I couldn't have imagined how long I would stay in Julia's apartment, out of a strange sense of loyalty, before I broke down and moved to Coconut Grove and took a job as an administrative assistant in a law firm, perhaps not so unlike the one Mr. Defonte had worked in. I couldn't have imagined that, after my father pled out and was sentenced to fifteen years, I would have flown all the way to Nevada to see him in jail, to tell him that his daughter was dead and our mother might as well be, to tell him that I missed him, that I would never forgive him, that he could fuck his fucking postcards, and not be able to get past the entrance. In fact, I couldn't even get out of the rental car. I sat in the parking lot for hours, blasting the Kingsmen CD I'd brought along, the postcards tucked into the glove compartment, before driving away. For the first ten miles I convinced myself that I was doing preliminary surveillance, that I would be back. I wondered if my husband would be consoled by the fact that the lies I told him were nothing compared with the ones I sometimes told myself. No, none of that seemed possible, as I watched Mrs. Defonte and Don Giovanni sing in a way that made my insides tremble.

The Commendatore came back to Don Giovanni in the form of a statue. The singer was painted silver and wore a helmet and a cape made of chain mail; he reminded me of the Tin Man from *The Wizard of Oz*. Even after I'd seen the whole opera, I kept willing Don Giovanni to not laugh in the graveyard, to not invite the Commendatore to dinner. *Run away*, I would whisper in the back row. *Just run away.* He never did, of course, and it wouldn't have changed anything if he had.

# LESSONS

# 1.

There are four of them.

Dana, Jackie, Pinky, and Cora are cousins. Pinky is also Dana's little brother. They call themselves the Gorillas because all gangs need a name—see Hole-in-the-Wall Gang, Stopwatch Gang, Winter Hill Gang—and also because they wear gorilla masks during their holdups. They are criminals, but they still have rules: no hostages, small scores, never stay in one town for more than a week. It's late summer and they're roving through the Midwest, from motel to motel, making just enough to keep going. Dana watches the impossibly flat landscapes of Lafayette and Oneida pass through the car window and wonders how they all ended up here. Why didn't they go to school and get regular jobs and get married and live in houses? The short answer: they are a group of people committed to making life as hard as possible.

Cora says they need to think bigger. No more knocking over delis and drugstores and dinky banks. They need to do a real heist. There are millions to be made, if they could just grow some balls. Jackie has simpler desires. She wants a boyfriend and a set of acrylic nails. Pinky is thirteen and wants to build a robot. Dana is more about what she doesn't want, as in: she doesn't want anyone to go to jail or die.

In L.A., a gang of female bank robbers have been making headlines. They wear Snow White masks and carry semiautomatics. Witnesses have reported them doing tricks with their guns during heists. They're rumored to be retired Romanian acrobats. Naturally, the press loves them. They've been nicknamed the Go-Go Girls.

"Why aren't we ever on TV?" Cora complains one night. They're in a motel in Galesburg. They have plans for the Farmers & Mechanics Bank on Main Street. Dana lies on one of the musty twin beds; her cousins are curled up on the other. Cora is green-eyed and lean with cropped auburn hair, like Mia Farrow in *Rosemary's Baby*. Jackie is shaped like a lemon drop. Her dark, wide-set eyes remind Dana of a well-meaning cow. Pinky is working on his robot in the bathroom. He's been collecting materials from gas station and motel Dumpsters: pins, wires, batteries, little black wheels. Earlier, Dana stood in the doorway and watched him screw two metal panels together. He sat cross-legged on the floor, his lips puckered with concentration. The overhead light flickered and buzzed. The spaces between the shower tiles were dark. She'd never seen him work so hard on anything before.

"Those are the kind of people who end up in shoot-outs with the police," Dana tells Cora. The Go-Go Girls have just stolen two million in diamonds from a bank in Beverly Hills. Dana picks up the remote and changes the channel to a cooking show. A woman is finishing a dessert with a blowtorch. Dana closes her eyes and listens to Pinky rattle around in the bathroom. Did they want a shoot-out with the police? She considers the Dalton Gang and John Dillinger. Is that what they want, to bleed to death on the street? The room is hot. The smell of burning rubber wafts through the bathroom door. No, she decides. No, it is not.

There is a river in Elijah, Missouri, that always appears in her dreams. They all grew up in Elijah. In this river they learned to float. Dana would stare up at the clouds and imagine they were spaceships or trains. In this river they would dive and search the bottom for smooth, flat stones. In real life it's a slender, slow-moving river, but in her dreams it's as wide as the Mississippi and silver, as though it's made of melted-down coins. From the shore she sees a raft with no one on it. She wants to get on the raft, but doesn't know how.

That night she wakes sweaty and breathless. She sits up. Pinky is next to her, asleep on top of the covers. He's rangy and sharp-elbowed. His arms are folded under his head. His mouth is pink and sticky from chewing red hots. She touches his pale hair—towheaded, her father used to say—and feels heat rising from his scalp. Outside, she hears rain falling. She lies back down. She tells herself to go to sleep. She tells herself to stop dreaming.

In the morning, they case the Farmers & Mechanics

Bank. They drive around the block twice in their Impala and then park at the pizza place across the street. To their left is a small roundabout with a patch of green and two withered trees in the center. It's called Central Park, which makes Dana think of the real Central Park in New York City, a place she will probably never see. A truck rattles past. The exhaust pops and Dana twitches in her seat. Cora is driving. Dana is sitting next to her. Jackie and Pinky are in the back and of course her brother is trying to wind two wires together. Dana imagines that when the Go-Go Girls case, it's all high-tech, with thermal imaging binoculars and fancy cameras. They just have their eyes.

They watch people come and go from the bank. They consider the flow of traffic on the street. They send Pinky in to pretend he's filling out a deposit slip. In Central Park, an American flag snaps in the breeze. A church bell calls out the hour. The bank is unassuming, just a brick building with tinted windows. When Pinky returns to the car, he gives a report on the interior layout, the number of tellers, and the points of exit and entry. According to him, there are only two tellers and they're both fat and slow. Dana watches a young woman emerge from the bank; a white envelope is tucked under her arm and she's holding a little boy by the hand. It startles Dana to think that the course of your life could depend on when you decide to cash a check or buy a roll of quarters.

"This one is going to be a breeze," she says.

"Where's the fun in easy?" Cora replies. She turns on

the radio and surfs until she finds the news. Tornadoes are in the forecast. Last night one of the Go-Go Girls was spotted at a nightclub in Malibu. There was a big chase with the police. Naturally, she escaped.

"A nightclub!" Cora slaps the steering wheel. "She was probably sitting in some guy's lap. She was probably drinking champagne."

"Champagne gives me a headache," Jackie says from the back.

"That's because you've never had the good stuff," Cora tells her.

"How would you know what the good stuff is?" Jackie replies.

At the motel, they clean their guns. Except for Pinky, who locks himself in the bathroom. They can hear him banging around in there. It sounds like he's acquired a hammer and a drill. Dana doesn't know where he could have gotten those things.

"He really wants to finish that robot before we leave town," she says.

"What if someone has to pee? Or take a shower?" Cora asks. "What then?"

"Your brother is so weird," Jackie says.

Their guns are old Smith & Wesson revolvers. They wipe them down with the white face towels they found in the motel room. Afterward they take out their gorilla masks and line them up on a bed. Black synthetic fur surrounds the rubber faces. The mouths are open, showing off plump pink tongues and fangs. They put the masks on. They pick up their guns and point them at each other. They aren't loaded, so they pull the triggers and listen to the hollow click. *Bang*, Dana whispers into the sweet-smelling rubber. She can see a bullet flying from the chamber and pinging her right in the forehead. She can see it burrowing into her brain. When people get shot in the movies, they flail and scream and stagger. Sometimes they even pretend to be dead and then come back to life. But that's not what it would be like at all, Dana thinks. She imagines it's just like turning out a light.

# 2.

In Elijah, they lived on a farm. The property held two gray houses, a chicken coop, and a dilapidated barn. The metal skeletons of cars rusted in the front yard. The barn was filled with dust and moldy straw. On the edge of the property, a small cross made from sticks had been pushed into the ground. It was a grave, but Dana never knew who it belonged to.

The mothers—her and Pinky's, Cora and Jackie's—were both the same: long-faced women scrubbed free of dissent and desire. Dana never heard either of them make a joke or sing. One of her earliest prayers was asking God to not let her end up like them. Cora and Jackie's father was gone. Years ago, he had driven away in the middle of the night. Dana remembered him being like lightning cracking in the sky, quick and mean. Her own father was stern but quiet, the kind who didn't need to raise his voice to incite fear. Once, during a homeschooling lesson, she learned 95 percent of the ocean was unexplored and thought her father must be like that, too: filled with dark, unseen caverns. Sometimes she longed for a father that popped and exploded like Cora and Jackie's had. At least then you knew what he was capable of.

Little was actually farmed on the farm. Her father didn't believe in working for pay. That was the government's system, he said. They were sovereign citizens. They ate homemade bread, snap beans that grew on vines, peppers, collards, and venison; they drank water that came from a well. They had chickens and a milk cow and a white goat. By the time the girls were seven, they knew how to handle a gun. They could hit the center of a bull's-eye. They could shatter the clay pigeons Dana's father tossed into the air. Every Sunday they had target practice because that was God's day and He would want them to be prepared. Cora always had great aim. Pinky never liked the shooting. He got his nickname from the way he flushed whenever he fired. He didn't like the weight of a gun in his hands. He didn't like the noise. He knew better than to say these things in front of his father, of course, but he told Dana when they were alone. She would lick her index finger and wipe dirt from his face and tell him that he would get used to it in time.

Once, when Dana was thirteen and Pinky was eight, their father took them turkey hunting. They were instructed to climb a tree and stay put until he called. From the branches of a chestnut oak, they watched him crouch in the tall grass and lure the turkey with a whistle. The bird moved slowly through the woods. Fall leaves crunched under its scaly gray feet. When it appeared, its tail feathers were spread into a beautiful rust-colored fan. Dana thought he looked big and regal, and for the first time the gap between what she knew and what the animal knew seemed cruel. It took only one bullet for the turkey to fall, heavy and silent as a sack of grain. Pinky put his hands over his eyes. Dana rubbed his back. When their father called, she hesitated. She pretended they were invisible in the tree. He kept calling, but his voice never sparked with anger. It wasn't patience, though. Dana understood that it was something else. When they finally went to him, he rolled the turkey over and showed where the bullet had gone in. He made them kneel beside the bird and touch the hole. It was gummy and warm. He told them fear of death was their greatest human weakness. He pulled a brown feather, the end tipped with white, from the turkey's tail and stuck it in Dana's hair.

The winter the girls turned eighteen, everything changed. A notice came in the mail. No one had paid taxes on the farm in decades and now the government was saying it owned the land. Her father tore up the first notice, because he didn't believe in taxes, but they kept coming.

Dana saw the envelopes stamped with *URGENT* that he brought home from the P.O. Soon they had just sixty days to pay. That was when their training became serious. They had target practice daily. They had drills where they would run along the perimeter of the property, rifles in hand. Even Pinky had to come. He always lagged behind the girls. Dana worried about him slipping on the ice and shooting himself in the foot. They would go out bundled in parkas and leather gloves and hunting caps, their breath making white ghosts in the air. After the first hour her arms would burn from the weight of the gun, but she would keep going. They were given a pair of binoculars and told to look out for strangers. Every night their father waited up in the kitchen for something to happen, for someone to come. Every night they recited a prayer that was meant for the eve of battle: *His days are as a shadow that passeth away / touch the mountains, and they shall smoke / Cast forth lightning, and scatter them*. During a snowstorm, Dana said she didn't see how anyone from the government could find them in this weather, and her father pointed out that snowfall could give the enemy perfect cover. That night, he asked her to wait up with him. He kept opening the front door and looking outside. Snow gusted into the house and padded the hallway with white. Flecks of ice got stuck in his dark eyebrows and hair. He showed her a pamphlet newspaper called *The Embassy of Heaven*, which had a Bible quote on the cover: "Do not suppose that I have come to bring peace to the earth." He said he had been writing to the newspaper and asking for help.

"Help with what?" They were sitting at the kitchen table. A rifle lay across his lap. Last week he'd torn out the landline and now a bundle of red and green wires dangled from the kitchen wall. They had a radio that got two stations, local news and gospel music; in the background she could hear the drone of an organ. She kept telling herself that the tax notices and her father's new habits would all pass eventually, like a hunting season.

"With the soul of this land," he told her. "With the soul of this family."

They'd turned the generator off for the night and the kitchen was cold. Dana had wrapped herself in a wool blanket. The room was lit by an oil lamp. In the half-dark, she could see how much her father's face had changed. The crescents under his eyes had hollowed out; his pupils looked darker, his cheekbones and chin sharper. His skin carried the sheen of a light sweat, even though it was freezing outside. The surface was falling away. She was finally seeing what lay beneath.

No one from the bank or the government ever came to Elijah. The snow kept falling. The river stayed frozen. By February the notices had stopped appearing in the mail. It seemed they had been forgotten. Still things did not go back to the way they were before. Dana's father thought it was a trick. He started working on a secret project in the barn. His face kept changing. At night she could hear her parents arguing and sometimes Dana would find her mother crying as she collected eggs from the chicken coop or squeezed milk from the cow. Both the mothers seemed exhausted by the vigilance they'd been required to keep. They lost the energy for homeschooling. When they gave the children their schoolbooks and sent them away, Dana's father didn't notice.

Of course, the children weren't really children anymore. There was only so much time they could spend shooting skeet and patrolling the property and flipping through musty textbooks. The idle time sparked a curiosity they had never felt before; it was as though they had each swallowed an ember and now it sat simmering in their stomachs. One afternoon Cora had this idea to wait on the road for a car to pass. They had some sense of what the outside world was like. They had accompanied Dana's father on trips to the farm store and the P.O. in West Plains. Once a month they went with the mothers to Fairfield's Discount Grocery, just a few miles down the road in Caulfield. Every fall they drove to visit Dana's grandparents, who had a computer and a TV, in Arkansas. But they had never done anything on their own, just the four of them.

After an hour of waiting, a truck rolled by and they hitched a ride to Miller's One Stop in Tecumseh. They wandered the dusty gas station aisles. Under the glare of fluorescent lights, Dana stared at the rows of Cokes and the freezer full of ice-cream sandwiches. Before they hitched a ride back, Cora pocketed a tube of Chapstick and a plastic comb. At home, they mashed the Chapstick into Pinky's hair and then combed it so it stood upright.

On another outing, they discovered that, five miles beyond the gas station, there was a town with a movie theater and a liquor store. The theater had an old-fashioned marquee and two screens. One of the films was always R-rated. The girls started talking the liquor store owner into selling them cigarettes; Pinky was the lookout. They would smoke behind the store and then toss the butts into a field. Once, they let Pinky smoke. He coughed and dropped the cigarette and Cora flicked his ear. They were always back well before dark. Their parents didn't seem to know they'd been gone, or catch the strange smells they brought home. The farm was more than two hundred acres, and Dana figured they thought their children were out on the land, like they'd always been. But their children were learning quickly. They were learning that the outside world and the pleasures it held weren't so bad. They were learning that they had never really believed in God; they had only ever believed in fear.

After they stole a map of American highways from the gas station, they spent hours sitting on the floor of Pinky and Dana's room, tracing the lines out to California and Oregon and Florida.

"Here." Cora lay on her side and pointed at San Luis. She had been eating sugar cubes from a cardboard box and her fingertip glistened. "That's where we should go."

Jackie was interested in traveling south, to New Orleans or Fort Lauderdale, but Cora said those places were too hot. Dana was intrigued by the small patchwork of northern states. They had studied geography during home-schooling, but now they were looking at the map in an entirely new light, as being full of places they might one day go.

"Too cold," Cora said when Dana touched the hook of land extending out of Massachusetts.

"Do you promise to take me with you?" Pinky asked. He didn't look his age, thirteen. He could have passed for ten or eleven. He reminded Dana of a rabbit; he had the same nervous nature and quick-beating heart. He never requested any particular place. He just wanted to make sure he wasn't left behind.

"We'll see." Cora ran her finger along the edge of California.

"Of course we'll take you," Dana said. He wasn't cut out for life in Elijah. It was too rugged, with the target practice and the long winters and the dead animals. She didn't yet know that he would be even more ill-prepared for the life she and her cousins would choose.

One night, in the early spring, they packed a single suitcase, hitched a ride to West Plains, and kept going. That was six months ago. Their parents never came look-ing for them, or if they did, they must not have looked very hard. Maybe they thought their children had fallen in with the government or the devil and were beyond hope. Or maybe they just didn't know how to search.

At first Dana thought leaving Elijah meant getting away from how things were on the farm, but now she thinks the past is like the hand of God, or what she imagines the hand of God would be like if God were real: it can turn you in directions you don't want to be turned in. They are still in a battle with the laws of the land. The laws that say they shouldn't steal or point guns at people. And she feels the same resistance to these laws that her father must have felt toward paying taxes. Why not do these things? she found herself thinking. Who is going to stop us?

Their first robbery was at a feed-and-grain store. They wanted money to buy a used car. It was so simple. They had stolen a shotgun from the bed of a truck they'd hitched in. All they had to do was walk inside. Dana told the teenage boy behind the counter to empty his register because that was a line she'd heard in one of those R-rated movies. She called him a cocksucker, too, since criminals seemed to say that all the time and she wanted him to know that she was to be taken seriously.

The boy gave them everything he had. Feed-and-grain stores aren't used to being robbed.

# 3.

The night before they hit the bank, Pinky tests his robot in the parking lot. Dana is the only one interested enough to watch. The floodlights are on; tiny bugs hover around the glow. The robot is covered in a pillowcase. It stands on the black asphalt like a ghost. Dana is smoking one of Jackie's cigarettes. She doesn't smoke much anymore, but it's the night before a job and that always makes her nervous. Once the thing is started, there's no sense in worrying because it's done, it's over. You can't rewind. But being on the edge, that's the hardest part. It's like standing in front of a burning building and knowing that it won't be long before you have to walk inside.

She sits on the ground and watches her brother peel away the pillowcase. The robot looks like a kid's science project. It has a round silver head and black buttons for eyes, an economy-size tomato soup can for a body, and large plastic suction cups for feet. It doesn't have any arms. Dana realizes that, for some reason, whenever she thinks of a robot, the first thing that comes into her mind are its arms.

"What do you think?" Pinky says.

"Nice work." Dana flicks the cigarette into the lot.

He tweaks some wires and the robot starts lurching in Dana's direction. It squeaks and sighs. A suction cup slips forward. It's working! She can't believe it. She stands up and begins to applaud. She feels proud of her brother for building something. For finding a way to escape his circumstances.

The robot takes one full step before toppling to the ground. The eyes pop off and slide under a car. The head gets dented. Pinky rights it and adjusts the wires, but he can't bring it back to life. Dana stops clapping. She sits down on the sidewalk.

He carries the robot over to her. "Do you want to hold it?"

"Sure." She holds it away from herself. It's surprisingly light.

"On TV people build robots that can talk." Pinky licks his lips.

"It probably takes a lot of practice," she says.

An old woman with flame-red hair shuffles past and disappears into a motel room. Above them Dana hears slamming doors.

"I don't want to leave," Pinky says. "I want to stay here and keep practicing."

"You want to stay in Galesburg?"

Pinky tells her that whenever they leave a place, he worries they won't make it to the next town. He worries the car will break down and no one will give them a ride and they'll starve to death or get heatstroke or something equally horrible. He's breathless. His eyes are glassy. She pictures his rabbit heart pulsing under his ribs. Probably leaving him in Galesburg would be the best thing for him, though she knows she could never do such a thing. She was the one who took him away from the farm and now she has to live with the consequences.

She gives the robot back to him. She doesn't tell him that if they die, it won't be from starving to death in their car. Instead she says everything is going to be fine, just like she used to in Elijah. No one is going to die. Soon he'll have all the time in the world to build a new robot.

"Does this one have a name?" she asks.

"Donald." He squeezes the robot's metal stomach and asks Dana what she thought their father was building in the barn.

Dana shrugs. She's never given much thought to what he was doing. She just remembers looking out her window and seeing him trudge into the mouth of the barn at dawn and not emerging until after dark. His skin would be caked in dust, straw caught in his hair. But mainly she had been preoccupied with figuring out how to live her own life, with how to spend her time. Dana wonders if her father is still working on his project in the barn, whatever it was. She imagines going back to Elijah one day and finding him a shrunken old man, and feels an ache shoot through her chest.

"I snuck in there once and watched him." Pinky describes pliers and cords and strips of metal. He talks about smelling smoke and seeing tiny silver sparks. "I think he was building a robot. I think that's what he wanted to do."

Dana looks at her brother and feels woozy. She never should have taken him along. It was a game at first, but now it's something much more serious and he is becoming an attachment she doesn't need.

"You know what they say in the movies?" she asks him.

"What?"

"They say you have to be cool." She can see a man in a

ponytail delivering the line, but can't remember which movie it's from.

"Okay." He's staring at the ground. She can tell she's not getting through.

"Say it to me."

He keeps hugging the robot. In his arms it looks like a heap of trash. It's only recently occurred to Dana that some people might call what she did—taking her brother away from their parents—kidnapping.

"Be cool," he tells her without looking up.

"You got it," she says.


# 4.


Dana was questioned by the police only once. It didn't have anything to do with the Gorillas. Rather, she was a witness to a hit-and-run. This was two months ago, in Jefferson City. She had just walked out of a bank the Gorillas were casing and was waiting to cross the street. A car ran a red light and struck a girl on a bicycle. The girl was dead by the time the ambulance came. Dana could remember the twisted handlebars and the crushed bell. She could remember the peculiar angle of the girl's torso and her open eyes. Her lips were parted. Her teeth were straight and white. She was still wearing her helmet. She looked like a life-size doll someone had left in the street. Pedestrians gathered. The police were called. Dana tried to slip away, but someone identified her as a witness and she was taken down to the station. She got to ride up front with the officer. She wondered what Cora or Jackie would think if they saw her, if they would think she had turned on them.

At the station, the officer brought her a cup of coffee. He was handsome, with his broad shoulders and gelled hair. So this is the lair of the enemy, Dana thought as they settled into an interrogation room. She held the warm foam cup with both hands. If only this officer knew what she had done, what she was going to do, she would not be answering questions over coffee. There would be handcuffs and threats. She figured that one day he would see her face on the news and feel like a dolt.

He asked her the usual questions: what she'd seen, if the light had been red, if she'd gotten a look at the driver, if she remembered the license plate. She answered honestly. She hadn't seen anything but the collision itself, hadn't taken in anything but the shock of the crash. She didn't mention that she hadn't been paying closer attention because she'd been busy imprinting the interior of the bank onto her brain.

"Do you need someone to identify the body?" Dana asked. She surprised herself with the question.

"You knew her?" The office frowned. He pulled in his chin and a little roll of fat appeared.

He had mentioned the girl was a college student. Dana muttered something about being classmates and seeing her around campus. She didn't know what had come over her. She had never seen a dead body before and up until then, that was A-okay. But she had been gripped by an urge she could not recognize or understand, only follow.

"Her parents are coming in from Chicago," the officer said. "We could save them the grief."

Dana sighed. Didn't he know there was no saving anyone any grief?

They took an elevator down to the morgue and passed through a cool, shadowed hallway. They stopped in front of a dark window. Dana could hear music coming through the glass. It was faint. A Michael Jackson song. For a moment, she imagined the medical examiner moonwalking around the autopsy room. The officer asked if she was ready. She nodded. A light came on.

The girl was lying on a coroner's table. She was naked, which alarmed Dana. It didn't seem right for her to be uncovered; someone had been careless. Her breasts were small and her knees seemed too big for her body. Her eyes were closed. Her hair looked wet and sleek. The blood had been cleaned away. Dana wondered where her bicycle helmet was. She couldn't believe this was the same girl she'd seen sprawled out on the street. It looked like her body had been replaced by a fake. How could these parents from Chicago identify their daughter with any kind of certainty? Maybe that was what happened when you died, Dana thought. Your real body went one place and a replica was provided for the rituals. And if that were true, where did the real bodies go? Someplace nice? Probably not.

"So is it her?" the officer said.

"What?" Dana turned from the window.

"Is she your classmate? Do you know her name?"

"It's not her," Dana said.

"What do you mean it's not her?" The officer frowned again. He was getting less attractive by the minute.

"I made a mistake," she said.

"Who makes that kind of mistake?" For the first time she noticed the gun holstered to his hip.

Dana wasn't afraid to just tell the officer the truth. After all, she hadn't broken any laws, that he knew of.

"Look, I wanted to see a body. I wanted to know what it would be like." She thought of that turkey in Elijah strolling through the woods one minute and still the next.

The officer said she could show herself out.

# 5.

At first everything goes perfectly at the Farmers & Mechanics Bank. They are all in their gorilla masks. Cora is pointing her gun at the tellers. Dana is aiming hers at the handful of customers who had the misfortune of being in the bank. They are crossed-legged on the floor; they have been ordered to sit on their hands, like elementary schoolers who can't stop hitting each other. Dana tries to ignore the little girl with braided hair. Pinky is guarding the door. Jackie, the getaway driver, is idling around the corner. Dana watches one teller load bricks of money into a bag. He has red hair and a mustache. The other teller is a woman. She's used so much hair spray, her hair doesn't budge when she whips her head left then right. Her lips are slick with pink, her lashes clumped with mascara. There's no sign of the fat, sluggish tellers Pinky described, but it looks like these two will do just fine.

It's the woman who fucks everything up. They see her hand slide under the counter and know she's going for the alarm. Cora shouts at her—*Hands in the air*—but the woman doesn't listen. Pinky is pacing by the door and pawing his rubber face. Dana takes small, quick breaths behind her gorilla mask. *Be cool*, she whispers, but it sounds artificial and weak. Stronger words are needed. She just doesn't know what they are.

The gunshot stops everyone. The mustached teller stops putting money in the bag. Pinky stops pacing. The customers stop squirming. The female teller is clutching her left eye. Blood seeps between her fingers. Cora's gun is still raised. It takes Dana more time than it should to understand that one of the Gorillas has just shot a bank teller in the face.

Her hands are numb. She concentrates on not dropping her gun. She thinks she's going to suffocate behind the mask.

"Give us our money." Now Cora is aiming at the other teller. His shirtsleeves are drenched in sweat. He goes back to heaving cash into the bag.

A woman in cowboy boots raises her hand. Her mouth is open, but she's not saying anything. She's pointing at something by the door. Dana turns and there's Pinky, slumped against the wall. He's kneading his gorilla mask in his hands. The customers and the tellers and the security cameras are all taking in his face. They are memorizing it. They are branding it onto their brains like Dana did with the interior of that bank in Jackson City.

"He is in such deep shit." Cora is waving her gun. She swivels toward Dana. "Can't you do something?"

But Dana can't. If she were a Go-Go Girl, then maybe she could, but she is just herself. The female teller is hunched over the counter and whimpering. She sounds like the wild dog Dana's father once had to shoot in Elijah. He kept coming onto their property, frothy and snarling, but once he had a bullet in him, he was docile as a lamb. Blood is still squirting through her fingers, as though her hand is a dam that's about to give. She's blinded at best. In the distance, Dana hears a siren. She looks at Cora and her cousin nods. They run for the exit. She pauses only to yank Pinky up by his shirt collar. He drops his gorilla mask on the sidewalk, but right then it doesn't matter. All that matters is diving into the waiting Impala. Of course Jackie wants to know what happened and where's the money and why isn't Pinky wearing his mask. Cora tells her to shut up and drive. They blast out of Galesburg. It's nearly dusk. The sun looks like it's setting the sky on fire.

They drive through the night. Pinky is up front, next

to Jackie. Dana and Cora are in the back. The window is cracked and Jackie is chain-smoking. They are heading to a little town called Wapello. They think it will be a good place to lie low, but soon Pinky's face will be all over the news and there will be no lying low from that.

"He can't stay with us anymore," Cora hisses in the backseat.

Dana just shakes her head. He could get plastic surgery, she thinks. A crazy idea. She gazes at her brother's profile. They are on a dark, straight highway. A little slicing, a little rearranging. She thinks of how handsome he could be.

On the radio, they hear that one of the Go-Go Girls has been shot in the stomach. She fell behind during a getaway. The officer who shot her said that he meant to hit her shoulder. Turns out that she wasn't an acrobat or Romanian. Just a girl from Minnesota.

"This is the problem with being famous," Dana announces to the car. "It makes everyone want to kill you."

No one says anything. Not even Cora. Dana leans her head against the window. As they're passing signs for Kirkwood, she thinks of the girl at the morgue and her parents in Chicago. She wonders if the cop ever tells her story, about the woman who conned him into checking out a dead body. If anyone ever tells her story.

Tornadoes are still in the forecast. A few times Dana thinks she sees a big black funnel moving toward them in the night. She thinks she hears that locomotive sound and feels the ground shake. She imagines being swept away. But there is nothing coming for them. Not yet. There is only this highway and this car and this darkness. She leans forward and squeezes her brother's elbow. He doesn't move, doesn't look at her. The remaining Gorilla masks are piled in his lap. He knows he's in a world of trouble.

They stop for gas and Dana makes Jackie hand her the car keys. When she says she wants to be sure no one gets left behind, Cora gives her a look. Pinky needs to use the bathroom. Dana stands outside and jingles the keys. She can see her parents hearing about Pinky on the radio. She can see them turning up the volume and leaning in close. Maybe they are being kept company by a robot made of soup cans and chicken wire, or maybe they are alone. Through the bathroom door, she hears the toilet flush. Her brother takes his time washing his hands.

When they're all back in the car, Cora passes her a note written on a paper napkin. *We are leaving him at the next fucking gas station!* it says in jagged black letters. Dana crumples the note and drops it on the floor. She slumps back and something crunches under her sneaker. She peers between her knees. It's the robot. Pinky got one of the eyes glued back on. If she tilts her head the right away, the metal gleams and she can tell herself it's their treasure, their loot. She thinks about rescuing the robot from the floor and giving it to her brother. She thinks about doing him that kindness. Instead she nudges the robot under the driver's seat and then feels sad about it. Poor Donald. She has to remind herself that robots don't have feelings. All these little choices that push her closer to something she's not sure she wants.

They pass a billboard with the slogan WANT A BETTER WORLD? It's too dark for Dana to see what's being advertised, but she guesses it's something religious. Of course she wants a better world. Who wouldn't want that? A world where everyone was like Pinky, pure and soft and full of dreams. Or she could just do things differently when it came to those small choices. She could give her brother the robot. She could throw her gun in a river. These could be her lessons. It's right there for her, that better world. She barely has to go looking.

Dana knows this, just as she knows that this is not the day she will find it.

ACROBAT

The day my husband left me, I followed a trio of acrobats around the city of Paris. The whole time my husband had been talking—telling me, presumably, why he was leaving—I was watching these acrobats do backflips and handstands in synchrony, an open violin case at their feet. They wore black masks over their eyes and white face paint. The little gold bells that hung from the sleeves of their red silk jumpsuits jingled like wind chimes. My husband and I were in the Jardin des Tuileries, sitting on a bench underneath a tree. We had come to Paris for the weekend, to revive our marriage. It was what the books and the couples counselor had recommended. The day he left was our last day there. We were, in fact, supposed to fly home that evening. We'd risen early to go to the Louvre and had gotten into a fight because he didn't want to wait in line to see the *Mona Lisa*.

"You have patience for things that I don't," he said while we were on the bench. "That's just the truth."

He said other things, too, but I was busy watching the acrobats perform in front of a fountain. They made a tower by standing on each other's shoulders and then leaped down, landing en pointe like dancers, their ballet slippers barely making a sound when they hit the pale dirt. *Now, that's teamwork*, I thought.

When I looked over at my husband, he wasn't sitting next to me. He was standing, his hands filling his pockets.

"So I guess that's that," he said.

"I guess so," I said. It was dawning on me that I might have missed something important.

"I'm going now."

"Wait a second," I said. "Surely we can still fly home together. Surely we're not that bad off." I checked my watch. It was noon. Our flight was only six hours away. Our luggage was packed and awaiting us in our hotel room and I was pretty sure I'd put my toiletries bag in my husband's suitcase. He told me he'd already canceled my ticket and left an envelope of money in our room to pay for a new one.

"It'll be better if we find our own way home," he said. "I explained that to you already."

"You said that just now?"

"Yes." He sighed. "Just now."

From the bench, I watched my husband disappear into a gaggle of French teenagers with backpacks sagging from their shoulders. I'd known this was coming. That the books and the counseling and the trip to Paris were all just passing time. But I hadn't expected it to happen right then, in the most romantic park in the most romantic city in all the world, or with so little drama.

I went back to the acrobats. When they folded up the violin case and marched out of the Jardin des Tuileries in a single-file line, I followed them. They wound expertly around clumps of pedestrians, never breaking formation, like ghosts walking among the living.

They went into the streets, past the Concorde, and down the Champs-Élysées. On the way, they stopped at a café and sat outside, smoking cigarettes and drinking espresso. They were there for over an hour. It was July; I imagined the acrobats were hot in their silk suits and face paint. I watched from a nearby food stand, eating a ham-and-cheese croissant. For once, I was grateful for my non-existent sense of style. My clothes couldn't have been plainer, a pale yellow sundress and black Teva sandals. A man in running shorts came up to me and said something in French that I could not understand. I shooed him away by flapping the wax paper my croissant had been wrapped in. Finally, one of the acrobats slipped euros underneath his saucer and then they all stood, dropped their white linen napkins onto their chairs, and filed out of the restaurant. The same acrobat who paid was at the head of the line. He also carried the violin case.

We went down the Champs-Élysées, past Ladurée, where I was momentarily distracted by a tower of yellow, pink, and purple macarons in the front window. A million different languages buzzed around me like radio static. My husband had refused to go to the Champs-Élysées because he said he would be revolted by the gross display of materialism. I looked at the shopping bags swinging from slender wrists and the mannequins posing in store windows and felt glad to be doing something that he would not. *So there*, I thought. Life goes on.

At the Arc de Triomphe, the lead acrobat stopped and opened the violin case. I watched them do the human tower trick again and then the leader pulled blue plastic balls from the case and they juggled. A couple had their picture taken with the two nonlead acrobats. The tourists were pale-haired, inelegant. They looked American, meaning they could have been my husband and me. The couple dropped coins into the violin case before leaving. The acrobats snapped up the case and moved along.

I followed them all the way to the Palais de Chaillot—where they preformed briefly, unable to command the attention of the people wading into the huge oblong fountain—and then the Eiffel Tower. If I lost sight of the acrobats for a moment, it was easy to find them in the crowd; all I had to do was listen for the singsong of the bells. By that time, I had tired of walking, and as I watched the acrobats do backflips and frontflips, I realized I didn't have a hotel reservation for the night. I had my passport, wallet, and guidebook in the satchel I was carrying. That was all. I sat down on a bench. A part of me was hoping that all this time, my husband had been following me around the arrondissements too. That, when I was least expecting it, he would sit down next to me. Or jump out from behind a tree and say, "Surprise!" That together we would still watch the lights of Paris grow smaller from the departing plane. I checked my wristwatch. It was five o'clock. Our flight—his flight—was an hour away. Soon my husband would be boarding, lifting his carry-on into the overhead compartment. He liked aisle seats. I hoped he didn't get one.

By the time the acrobats left the Eiffel Tower, dusk was falling, and I had become less concerned with being cautious. I followed close enough to see where sweat had seeped through their silk jumpsuits, forming shapes that looked like wings. They went to a small restaurant with a yellow awning called Florimond's, where they got a table inside. In my broken French, I asked the maître d' for a table in the same section. Both the acrobats and I sat facing the restaurant's front patio and the street. Two empty tables stood between us. I pretended to study the menu. I felt my knee and noticed my dress was missing a button. When I stole glances at the acrobats, they were all looking at menus and smoking.

I decided to order a big meal. I decided to eat until I felt like bursting. I started by asking for my own bottle of wine. As I sipped my first glass of wine, I felt something in the room change, like all the electrical currents had been moving in one direction and then suddenly started going in another. Or, as my husband would say, the "emotional weather" was different. He was always accusing my emotional weather of changing without warning. The forecast had predicted clear skies and then, out of nowhere, here came the rain clouds. Time after time, I tried to explain that I didn't have much control over my emotional weather, and viewed the local weatherman with newfound empathy whenever I saw him on the evening news. I stared at my hands as I thought of these things. These moments that pass for a life.

I heard a jingling and when I looked up, the lead acrobat was sitting across from me. I gasped and knocked over my wineglass. The acrobat righted the glass and mopped up the wine with a napkin.

"Merci," I said. I could see his dark eyes through the holes in the mask, which, up close, reminded me of the one Zorro wore in the movies. The white paint on his mouth had flaked away. I noticed the pinkish color of his lips.

"Pourquoi nous suivez-vous?" the acrobat said.

"Une minute." I took out my travel guide and flipped to the translation section.

"Why didn't you say so?" the acrobat said when he saw what I was doing. "We all speak English."

"I didn't want to assume," I said, by which I meant I didn't want to seem like some dumb American.

"I'll start over," the acrobat said. "Why are you following us?"

Naturally, I was at a loss for what to say.

"Don't get me wrong," he continued. "We're quite flattered. We've never had such a loyal fan before. But still we have to ask."

I glanced over at the other acrobats. They were huddled together, staring, and then, after they caught my eye, pretending not to stare. It was my habit to lie to strangers, because how would they know the difference? On the flight over, my husband and I ended up in different rows and I told the man sitting next to me that I was a geologist. Talking to someone who didn't know me, who couldn't separate the truth from the lie, always gave me the most ruthless sense of freedom. But today was a different kind of day.

"To tell you the truth, I was watching you perform while my husband was telling me something important and I missed what he was saying," I said. "That's the best answer I can give."

"Can't you just ask your husband to repeat himself?"

"Not exactly," I said. "I think he went home without me."

"And where's home?"

"America," I said. "Connecticut."

"I see," said the acrobat. He looked over at his comrades, then back at me. He said his name was Jean-Paul and invited me to sit at their table. I accepted. Jean-Paul informed the maître d' and carried over my wine bottle. He introduced me to the other acrobats, Alain and Dominique. They moved their chairs to make room, pushed their glasses together. With the face paint and the masks, I couldn't really tell the difference between Alain and Dominique. Both had light brown hair and greenish eyes. Jean-Paul I could distinguish because he was the tallest, with dark hair and dark eyes.

"This woman is alone in the city," Jean-Paul said once we were settled. The table was in a corner and I was sitting next to him, facing the street, Alain and Dominique across from us.

"Not anymore," Alain—or Dominique?—said. "Acrobats know how to treat their fans."

"There's so much competition now," Dominique—or Alain?—said. "Musicians, puppet shows, mimes. You practically have to set yourself on fire to get noticed."

"I love acrobats," I said, unsure if that was even really true. "I've loved acrobats ever since I was a child."

Our food arrived. All three of the acrobats had ordered coq au vin. We ate quickly and in silence. I was relieved that I wasn't the only one too hungry for polite conversation. After our plates had been cleared, Jean-Paul presented me with an open cigarette pack. I took one. It was slender and white. I'd never had a cigarette before. My husband was an environmental enthusiast and thought smokers were the scourge of the earth. He had actually used that word, "scourge." I inhaled deeply and didn't cough. I felt the smoke move through my chest like something alive.

"Would you like to go to a party tonight?" Jean-Paul asked.

"It's an acrobat party," Alain/Dominique added.

"We'd have to get you a costume," Jean-Paul said. "Or at least some face paint and a mask."

"I didn't know acrobats had their own parties," I said.

Jean-Paul explained that most acrobats in Paris were the children of acrobats, that it was a time-honored vocation. "We have our own networks," he said. "Our own social clubs."

I tried to imagine a crowd of people with painted faces and masks. "This isn't some kind of sex thing, is it?"

"Not at all," Jean-Paul said. "Or at least not usually."

I told them I was in. The acrobats clapped, their bells chiming. All the wine was gone. When the check came, I took out my Visa and slapped it down on the table. My card had a twenty-thousand-dollar limit. I always told my husband that I didn't need a card with such a high limit, but he said it was good for our credit to have so much power and to use it responsibly and, in any case, there might be an emergency. My husband had been right about that. I was having an emergency. I was the emergency. And I was glad to have power to burn.

After the bill had been settled, Jean-Paul took out a tube of white face paint and a tiny makeup brush. He moved his chair closer to mine, then leaned toward me and asked me to close my eyes. Without sight, noises were magnified: the soft hiss of a match being lit, dishes clattering, the distant, lilting wail of a siren. He used his fingers to paste the paint onto my face, over my eyelids and down the bridge of my nose. It felt like cold mud. He pressed my cheekbones as he swirled the paint upward. I imagined a white line moving up the center of my forehead and then fanning out like a breaking wave. I could not remember the last time my husband had touched my face. Before finishing, Jean-Paul evened out the job with the makeup brush, its bristles pricking my nostrils and the edges of my mouth.

Jean-Paul told me to open my eyes. I gazed into the compact mirror he held in front of me. Everything was white except for my eyelashes and eyebrows and pupils. When I grinned, my teeth looked yellow against my painted skin.

"Voilà!" he said.

At the table, the acrobats used the makeup brush and the compact mirror to touch up their own faces. Then we went to a costume store on Rue Eblé. Inside, the acrobats picked out a black masquerade mask lined with silver glitter and a black silk robe. I charged the costume on my Visa. Outside, in an alley, Jean-Paul helped slip the mask over my face and then tied the silk sash of the robe around my waist. His fingers were nimble, slender.

The party was in the Marais. We took the metro. We sat in a row, in our face paint and masks. People didn't stare as much as I had expected, as I had hoped. The only ones who really gave us a second look were children. The overhead lights flickered and hummed. When our stop came and we stood, I realized gum was stuck to the bottom of my sandal.

Aboveground, I followed the acrobats down Rue Saint Sébastien. There were restaurants with outdoor patios and nightclubs with neon signs nestled in the windows. The streets were made of beautiful stone. We walked single-file. I was at the end of the line. Once, I got distracted by a couple eating on a restaurant patio, another pale and inelegant pair, but I only had to listen for the bells to find the acrobats in the crowd. We turned onto a cobblestone side street. The stones looked wet even though it hadn't rained. We stopped outside a gray building with a little blue awning. We rang the buzzer and went inside.

When the elevator reached the sixth floor, we found the corner apartment open and people spilling into the hallway. They all had on white face paint, but some had blue stars ringing their eyes or a red joker's smile or yellow comets on their cheeks. Some wore jumpsuits, like my acrobats, others tights and tunics. A woman in a turquoise one-piece bathing suit, a beaded dolphin covering her stomach. A man in a floppy jester hat with bells. Everywhere was the sound of bells.

"This is the party," Jean-Paul said. He set the violin case down by the door. I followed him inside.

The apartment was bright and full. French pop music played on the stereo. The floors were gleaming hardwood.

At the other end of the room, a bay window looked out onto the street. People were standing elbow to elbow, shoulder to shoulder, knee to knee. I couldn't get a good look at the layout and décor. The apartment had been overrun by acrobats and their followers.

Jean-Paul, Alain, and Dominique spread out, shaking hands and slapping backs and waving to masked figures across the room. Right away, my Teva sandals made me feel like an impostor. I needed high heels or ballet slippers or even bare feet with crimson toenails. I wandered into the kitchen. Glass bowls filled with punch sat on granite counters, alongside champagne glasses and cocktail napkins. Tiny charms in the shape of acrobats dangled from the stems of the glasses. Costumed partygoers leaned against doorjambs, propped elbows on counters, talked in rapid-fire French. I had expected this party to be unique, a once-in-a-lifetime event, but it was the same as any other party, really, except everyone was masked and speaking a language I couldn't understand. I ladled some punch into a champagne glass and drank it. Then I walked around with the empty glass in my hand.

The fish tank in the living room attracted me. The tank was black and had fluorescent lights, but there was nothing inside except water and silver pebbles. I studied the spines of the books in a bookcase: titles on deep-space organisms and intergalactic travel and black holes. I wondered if the person who owned this apartment ever dreamed of astronauts. A woman with crystals glued to her cheek in the shape of a heart tried to talk to me, but I couldn't follow what she was saying. I just nodded until my neck hurt and the apartment felt airless. I pushed past a group of people wearing masks adorned with feathers and back into the kitchen. I filled my champagne glass and went out onto a small balcony with iron railings. It faced the same street as the bay window. Below, I saw the tops of heads and garbage can lids and slick stone streets. No one else was on the balcony and I couldn't talk to the people indoors. I hadn't seen Jean-Paul, Alain, or Dominique since we entered the party. I was starting to feel lonely for home. I went inside and slipped into a bedroom.

I sat on the edge of the bed. I stared at the black phone on the bedside table. It was an old-fashioned rotary, an antique possibly. I dialed my husband's international cell. I was surprised when he answered after the first ring.

"Hello," I said. "I didn't think you'd pick up."

"I'm in Amsterdam," he said. "My connection was delayed."

"Are you going back to Hartford? Back to the house?"

"Where else did you think I'd go?"

"I don't know." He had a brother who lived in upstate New York, a best friend from college in Des Moines. "Someplace I wouldn't come back to." I'd left the door cracked open and noise from the party seeped into the room.

"Where are you?" my husband asked.

"A party," I said. "I met some people after you left."

"Oh," he said.

"So do you think you should get the house?"

"Isn't that a little premature?"

"Leaving someone in a foreign country seems pretty final to me."

"Do *you* want the house?"

"I never liked that house," I said. "It was too dark. And the neighborhood was too quiet. It kept me up at night, it was so quiet. It short-circuited my nerves, it was so quiet."

"I like quiet."

"I know," I said. "I always hated that about you."

"Let's figure the house out when you get back." He paused. "When are you getting back?"

"I'm not sure." I pressed the receiver against my forehead and shut my eyes. I heard him ask me to not take so long between answers, because these international minutes were costing him a fortune. Finally I said I had a question for him.

"Shoot."

"When we were sitting on the bench this morning, you were saying something to me. Something important."

"I could tell you weren't paying attention," he said. "You kept looking over my shoulder."

"That's true," I said. "I was distracted. There were these acrobats."

"And now you're wondering what I said?"

"I was hoping you'd repeat it for me."

"We all have to live with our deficiencies."

"That's what you said?"

"No. That's what I'm saying now."

"What does that mean? That you're not repeating it for me?"

"There are consequences for the things we do. That's what I'm saying."

"Consequences?"

"Consequences."

"I don't believe in consequences. There's just what happens and what doesn't."

"I'm glad to hear you still sound just like yourself."

"Did you say that you loved me?"

"No."

"That you never really loved me?"

"No."

"That you'd met someone else?"

"Wrong again."

"That you're planning to kill me and collect my life insurance payout?"

"It's crossed my mind," he said. "But no."

I felt like beating my head against the wall until my nose was bloody. I asked why we kept trying for so long, why we even came to Paris, if we both knew we never really stood a chance.

"Because that's what you're supposed to do," he said. "You're supposed to keep working on your marriage."

It was awful to me, this idea that keeping a marriage together was like laying pipe or digging a ditch. But he

was right: it was what people had told us we were supposed to do. We had listened to sentences containing words
like "salvage" and "repair" and nodded dumbly, pretending
we didn't know any better. It was an affront to everyone
involved.

I leaned against the pillows and the headboard. I
breathed in deeply, but when I exhaled, no air seemed to
come out, like something inside me had eaten it. "How
was the flight out of Paris?"

"Turbulent."

"Did you miss me?"

"Not as much as I thought I would, to be honest."

"I don't miss you that much either."

I waited for him to say something else. I listened to his
breath on the line. For a moment, I thought I was on the
brink of profound clarity. I silently counted backward from
ten and when I hit zero, I hung up.

I lay on the bed for a while longer, my fingers gripping
the black silk of my robe. I blinked behind the mask. All
of a sudden, darkness replaced the knife-blade of light
that had been visible under the doorway. I went back to
the living room, forgetting my empty champagne glass
with its miniature acrobat charm on the comforter. The
apartment was dark. The music changed to techno, which
I hadn't heard since college. I hadn't liked it then, but now
it sounded okay. Someone activated a strobe light and white
beams cut across the room. People were dancing all over
the apartment, in their bells and sequins and feathers.

"Henri," Jean-Paul whispered in my ear. He had appeared behind me, his hands on my shoulders. "He went to the clubs in Monaco one summer and he's been obsessed with those lights ever since."

The lights beamed one way, and I saw into the kitchen, where Alain and Dominique were dancing with the woman in the dolphin bathing suit. The glass bowls on the counter looked like they were holding blood. It seemed everyone was smiling. Some of the smiles were painted on, of course, but I wanted to believe that everyone was smiling for real. I saw teeth and gums and tongues, just a glimpse here and a glimpse there, never enough to identify what belonged to who.

"Henri is from America originally," Jean-Paul continued. "Our favorite American import."

"I thought I was your favorite American import," I said, bumping against him. This was the first time I'd tried to flirt with anyone in years.

"But of course!" Jean-Paul said. He draped his arms around my neck. Intersecting white lights shot across the apartment. I put Jean-Paul's hands on my hips and we danced. We didn't dance close. We jumped up and down, left and right, knocking into other people. We held hands, and when we let go of each other, it was too dark for me to see if he was dancing with someone else or waiting for me to return, if he too was smiling. I let out a scream and felt a little thrill. I did it again and got the same rush. It was dark and I was masked and no one knew who I was or where I was going next or whether I was losing my mind or finding it.

When the song ended, Jean-Paul took my hand and led me out of the apartment. It was still pitch dark and no one could see that we were escaping. I marveled at all that could be gotten away with in the dark. Someone's life could fall apart—or together—without anyone noticing a thing. I thought of all the nights I lay beside my husband in bed and agonized about where my life was going, where it had gone, about being thirty-five and having not done much of anything. All those hours in darkness, a shadow life that was never revealed to him. I might as well have been robbing banks on the sly or having an affair.

Outside, I touched my cheeks and felt the paint smudge. When I pulled my hand away, there was white on my fingertips. I was sweating beneath my mask and robe. Jean-Paul broke into a light run, still holding my hand, his bells jingling, my sandals slapping the ground like Frankenstein feet.

"Where do you want to go?" Jean-Paul asked. We were running down a street lit by globular lamps.

I remembered the first thing I took an interest in when studying a map of Paris on the plane. I read about its history in the guidebook and charted its path on the map with my fingertip.

"To the river!" I said.

By the time we reached the Seine, we had given up on

running. We knew better than to feign being young and carefree for very long. The paint was making my face itch. I scratched the side of my nose. I had lost my sash and my robe billowed open. When I looked down at my sundress, it seemed unfamiliar, a stranger's clothes. The Seine stretched out before us, dark and endless. We took a small set of stairs down to the concrete sidewalk that lined one side of the river. The path was lit by goldish hanging lights. We walked along the river, underneath one of the bridges and past an empty bench. Jean-Paul smoked a cigarette and gave me drags. The concrete wall beside us insulated us from city sounds. For a long time, the bells were the only noise I heard.

"You forgot your case," I said when I realized he wasn't carrying it.

"It doesn't matter," he said. "One of the others will take it."

"How did you learn acrobatics?"

"I went to an acrobatics school in Normandy," he said. "I was taught by the same man who taught my father."

"It seems like it would get tiring, all that performing."

"I like having a job where I get to wear a mask all day."

When he asked what I did, I tried my best to explain my job as a forensic accountant. I worked in the offices of a divorce lawyer in Hartford and spent my days examining bank statements and stock portfolios, trying to figure out what really belonged to whom, where money had been hidden or lost or spent. I hoped the office would be understanding when I called to tell them I was extending my vacation.

"Once our office had a case where the wife had been grinding up tiny amounts of glass and mixing it into her husband's food for the last year of their marriage," I said.

"Maybe it's best your husband left when he did."

"Maybe so."

A riverboat, the bottom exploding with blue phosphorescent light, drifted past us; music and voices rolled across the water. When the quiet returned, I stopped walking. Jean-Paul faced me. I touched his shoulder, right where the silk rose into a little peak, with my paint-smudged fingers.

"Take off your mask," I said.

"Sorry," he said. "It's against the code."

I wondered what the mask was hiding, if he was elaborately scarred. "I'll take off my mask if you take off yours."

He smiled. "But I already know what you look like."

"You don't know my name. I never told any of you my name."

"I've already made one up for you," he said. "I do that when I meet people."

"And?"

"It's Sabine. What do you think?"

"Not even close."

I took off my mask and let my bathrobe fall onto the

concrete, the black silk pooling at my feet, and undid the straps on my sandals. It looked as though a wizard had evaporated, leaving behind everything but the body. I took one sweeping step toward the edge of the path and jumped into the water cannonball style, knees clutched to my chest like a terrified child.

I plunged beneath the water. I didn't open my eyes. I considered what might be resting under me: dead bodies with gnawed fingers and peeling skin, bottles, disposed-of murder weapons, coins, disintegrating love letters. I felt the gentle pressure of the current, the fabric of my dress sticking to my skin.

After I surfaced, I opened my eyes and slicked back my hair. I wiped my face and looked at the white paint bleeding across my hands. Jean-Paul was standing on the bank in his underwear and mask, his red jumpsuit and ballet slippers heaped on the concrete. He slipped into the river tentatively, as though the water was causing him pain.

When he reached me, he put his hand on the back of my head. I looked at his lips and nose and ears. His mask had slipped to the side and I saw one of his eyes. Whiteness had collected in the corner of it. I rubbed the remaining paint from his face with my fingertips. His mask and black hair made me think again of Zorro. I traced a Z on his bare stomach. I hoped another riverboat didn't pass through.

"Did anyone ever tell you that you look like Zorro?"

"What is Zorro?"

"It's not important."

"Do you have a place to stay tonight?"

"I want to take a train south. To the beaches. I want to see things." The idea of traveling south had come out of nowhere, but I liked the way the words sounded, the way they felt, as they left my mouth.

"But you'll need a place to dry off, change clothes, get some sleep."

"I could do that anywhere."

Jean-Paul gripped my waist and hoisted me out of the water. I made a V with my arms and he spun me around, his hands moving over my stomach and the small of my back. I saw the gray walls of the Seine and the cars and a person crossing a bridge. All the lit-up windows and the glowing peak of the Eiffel Tower. I tipped my head back and saw the red blink of a plane in the sky. And then he brought me back down.

ANTARCTICA

In Antarctica, there was nothing to identify because there was nothing left. The Brazilian station at the tip of the Antarctic Peninsula had burned to the ground. All that remained of my brother was a stainless steel watch. It was returned to me in a sealed plastic bag, the inside smudged with soot. The rescue crew had also uncovered an unidentified tibia, which might or might not have belonged to him. This was explained in a cold, windowless room at Belgrano II, the Argentinean station that had taken in the survivors of the explosion. Luiz Cardoso, the head researcher at the Brazilian base, had touched my shoulder as he spoke about the bone, as though this was information intended to bring comfort.

Other explanations followed, less about the explosion and more about the land itself. Antarctica was a desert. There was little snowfall or rain. Much of it was still unexplored. There were no cities. The continent was ruled by no one; rather, it was an international research zone. My brother had been visiting from McMurdo, an American base on Ross Island, but since it was a Brazilian station that had exploded, the situation would be investigated according to their laws.

"Where is the bone now? The tibia?" I'd lost track of how long it had been since I'd slept, or what time zone I was in. It felt very strange to not know where I was in time.

"In Brazil." His English was accented, but clear. It had been less than a week since the explosion. "It's not as though you could have recognized it."

We stood next to an aluminum table and two chairs. The space reminded me of an interrogation room. I hadn't wanted to sit down. I had never been to South America before, and as Luiz spoke, I pictured steamy Amazonian rivers and graveyards with huge stone crosses. It was hard to imagine their laws having sway over all this ice. It was equally hard to believe a place this big—an entire fucking continent, after all—had no ruler. I felt certain that it would only be a matter of time before there was a war over Antarctica.

"It's lucky the explosion happened in March." Luiz was tall with deep-set eyes and the rough beginnings of a beard, a few clicks shy of handsome.

"How's that?" My brother was dead. Nothing about this situation seemed lucky.

"Soon it will be winter," he said. "It's dark all the time. It would have been impossible for you to come."

"I don't know how you stand it." The spaces underneath my eyes ached.

My husband hadn't wanted me to come to Antarctica at all, and when our son saw where I was going on a map, he had cried. My husband had tried to convince me everything could be handled from afar. *You're a wife*, he'd reminded me as I packed. *A mother, too.*

"Did you know about your brother's work?" Luiz said. "With the seismograph?"

"Of course." I listened to wind batter the building. "We were very close."

I couldn't stop thinking about him as a boy, many years before everything went wrong: tending to his ant farms and catching snowflakes in his mouth during winter. Peering into a telescope and quizzing me on the stars. Saying tongue twisters—*I wish to wish the wish you wish to wish*—to help his stutter. We had not spoken in over a year.

Luiz clapped his hands lightly. Even though we were indoors, he'd kept his gloves on. I had drifted away and was surprised to find myself still in the room.

"You have collected your brother's things, such as they are. There will be an official inquiry, but you shouldn't trouble yourself with that."

"I'm booked on a flight that leaves in a week. I plan to stay until then."

"The explosion was an accident," he said. "A leak in the machine room."

"I get it." Exhaustion was sinking into me. My voice sounded like it was coming from underwater. "Nobody's fault."

I had flown from JFK to New Zealand, where I picked up a charter plane to an airstrip in Coats Land. There had been gut-popping turbulence, and from the window I could see nothing but ice. Luiz had been the one to meet me on the tarmac and drive me to Belgrano II in a red snow tractor. I'd packed in a hurry and brought what would get me through winter in New Hampshire: a puffy coat that reached my knees, a knit hat with a tassel, leather gloves, suede hiking boots. I'd had to lobby hard to come to Antarctica; the stations weren't keen on civilians hanging around. When I spoke with the director of McMurdo, I'd threatened to release a letter that said details of the explosion, the very information needed to properly grieve, were being kept from the victims' families. I knew Luiz was looking me over and thinking that the best thing I could do for everyone, including my brother, including myself, was to just go on home.

"Are there polar bears here?" I felt oddly comforted by the idea of a white bear lumbering across the ice.

"A common mistake." He drummed his fingers against the table. He had a little gray in his eyebrows and around his temples. "Polar bears are in the north pole."

"My brother and I were very close," I said again.


There was a time when that statement would have been true. We had been close once. During our junior year of college, we rented a house in Davis Square, a blue two-story with a white front porch. Our parents had died in a car accident when we were in middle school—a late spring snowstorm, a collision on a bridge—leaving behind the grandparents who raised us and an inheritance. My brother was in the earth sciences department at MIT; I was studying astronomy at UMass Boston (I was a year older, but he was on an accelerated track). Back then I thought I would never grow tired of looking at the sky.

When it was just the two of us, we did not rely on language. He would see me cleaning chicken breasts in the sink, and take out breadcrumbs and butter for chicken Kiev, our grandmother's recipe. After dinner, we watched whatever movie was on TV. *E.T.* played two nights in a row and *maybe it was an iguana* became something we said when we didn't know what else to do, because even though we had been close, we never really learned how to talk to each other. Sometimes we didn't bother with clearing the table or washing dishes until morning. We went weeks without doing laundry. My brother wore the same striped polos and rumpled khakis. I showed up for class with unwashed hair and dirty socks. His interest in seismology was taking hold. He started talking about P-waves and S-waves. Fault lines and ruptures. He read biographies on Giuseppe Mercalli, who invented a scale for measuring volcanoes, and Frank Press, who had land named after him in Antarctica, a peak in the Ellsworth Mountains.

It was at MIT that he met Eve. She was a theater arts

major. They dated for a semester and wed the same week they graduated, in the Somerville courthouse. I was their only guest. Eve wore a tea-length white dress and a daffodil behind her ear. She was lithe and elegant, with straight blond hair and freckles on the bridge of her nose. When the justice of the peace said "man and wife," she had called out "wife and man!" and laughed and then everyone started laughing, even the justice. I wasn't sure why we were laughing, but I was glad that we were.

There were three bedrooms in the house. It might have seemed strange, brother and sister and his new wife all living together, but it felt like the most natural thing. Our first summer, we painted the walls colors called Muslin and Stonebriar and bought rocking chairs for the porch. We pulled the weeds that had sprung up around the front steps. All the bedrooms were upstairs. When I was alone in my room, I played music to give them privacy. At dinner, I would watch my brother and Eve—their fingers intertwined under the table, oblivious—and wonder how long it would take them to have children. I liked the idea of the house slowly filling with people.

That fall, my brother started his earth sciences PhD at MIT. He kept long hours in the labs, and when he was home, he was engrossed in textbooks. Eve and I spent more time together. She lived her life like an aria—jazz so loud, I could hear it from the sidewalk; phone conversations that sprawled on for hours, during which she often spoke different languages; heels and silk dresses to the weekend farmers' market. She always wore a gold brace-let with a locket. I would stare at the oval dangling from her wrist and wonder if there was a photo inside. I helped her rehearse for auditions in the living room, standing on a threadbare oriental rug. I got to be Williams's Stanley Kowalski and Pinter's Max, violent and dangerous men. I started carrying slim plays around in my purse, like Eve did, even though I had no plans to write or perform; the act alone felt purposeful. I learned that her father was an economics professor and she had majored in theater to enrage him, only to discover that she loved the stage. I'd never met anyone from her family before.

One afternoon I went to see her perform in *The Tempest* at a community theater in Medford. My brother had been too busy to come. She was cast as Miranda. Onstage she wore a blue silk dress with long sleeves and gold slippers. In one scene, Miranda argued with her father during a storm; somewhere a sound machine simulated thunder. Everything about her carriage and voice worked to convey rage—"Had I been any great god of power, I would have sunk the sea within the earth . . ."—but for the first time, I noticed something was wrong with her eyes. Under the lights, they looked more gray than blue, and her gaze was cold and flat.

Afterward, we drank at the Burren. The bar was bright and crowded. A band was unpacking instruments from black cases. We jammed ourselves into a small table in the back with glasses of red wine. Eve was depressed about the production: the turnout, the quality of the lighting and the costumes.

"And the guy who played Prospero," she moaned. She had left a perfect lip print on the rim of her wineglass. "I would've rather had my own father up there."

When the waitress came around, she ordered another drink, a martini this time. She took an eyebrow pencil out of her purse and drew hearts on a cocktail napkin.

"What do squirrels give for Valentine's Day?" she asked.

I shook my head. My hands were wrapped around the stem of my glass.

"Forget-me-nuts." She twirled the pencil in her fingers and laughed the way she had during her wedding, only this time I caught the sadness in her voice that I'd missed before.

She put down the pencil and leaned closer. At the table next to ours, a couple was arguing. The band tuned their guitars. When she spoke, her voice was syrupy and low.

"Lee," she said. "I have a secret."

In Antarctica, I shared a bedroom with a meteorologist from Buenos Aires. Her name was Annabelle and she talked in her sleep. Every morning, I had a three-minute shower in the communal bathroom (it was important to conserve water). I took my meals in the mess hall, with its long tables and plastic trays and harsh overhead lights. I sat with the ten Argentinean scientists who worked at the base; we ate scrambled eggs and canned fruit and smoked fish. They spoke in Spanish, but I still nodded like I could follow. The five scientists from the Brazilian station always sat at their own table, isolated by their tragedy, which I understood. After my parents died, it took me months before I could carry on a conversation with someone who had not known them, who expected me to be young and sparkling and untouched by grief.

Four of the Argentinean scientists were women. They had glossy dark hair and thick, rolling accents. In Antarctica, I'd found that personalities tended to match the landscape, chilly and coarse, but these women were kind. There was a warmth between them, an intimacy, that made me miss being with Eve. They lent me the right clothes. They let me watch the launch of their meteorology balloon from the observation room, a glass dome affixed to the top of the station. The balloon was white and round, a giant egg ascending into the sky. In broken English, they told me what it was like during the darkness of winter: *The sun*, they said. *One day it's just not there. There are no shadows. You have very strange dreams.* They included me in their movie nights in the recreation room, which had a TV, a small library of DVDs, a computer, and a phone. Once it was *Top Gun*, another time *E.T.* Everything was dubbed in Spanish, and when I didn't get to hear the iguana line,

I started to cry. I didn't make a sound, didn't even realize it was happening until I felt the wetness on my cheeks. The women pretended not to notice.

I started wearing my brother's watch. No matter how much I cleaned the metal, it kept leaving black rings around my wrist. With my calling card, I phoned McMurdo, only to be told that the scientists who worked with my brother had departed in anticipation of winter; all they could offer was the date he left and that their reports indicated he'd been in good health. I started pestering Luiz for a meeting with everyone from the Brazilian station, with the hope that they had more to tell.

"An interview?" he'd asked, frowning.

"No." By then I'd been in Antarctica for three days, though I felt it had been much longer. "A conversation."

The day of the meeting, I dressed in thermals, snow pants, wool socks, fleece-lined boots, a hooded parka, and thick red gloves that turned my hands into paddles. I added a white ski mask that covered everything but my eyes. From Annabelle, I'd learned it was called a balaclava. She had given me a laminated sheet with a drawing of a human body. Arrows pointed to what kind of layer should cover each part, to avoid frostbite.

When I first stepped onto the ice, I felt like an astronaut making contact with the surface of the moon. I wandered around the trio of heated research tents and the buzzing generators and the snow tractors. The sky was blue-black; the period of twilight, which seemed to grow smaller each day, would soon begin. By April, Antarctica would be deep into winter and there would be no relief from the dark.

I found all five of the Brazilians in the middle research tent, standing by a long white table covered with black rocks. With the snowsuits and the balaclavas, it was hard to tell who was who, though I always recognized Luiz by his height. Some of the rocks on the table were the size of a fist; others the size of a grapefruit. One was as large as a basketball.

"Meteorites," Luiz said when he saw me looking. Apparently the ice in Antarctica preserved meteorites better than any climate in the world. His team had discovered ones that were thousands of years old.

I touched the basketball-size rock—sand-colored and banded with black—and remembered how much my brother had loved the moon rock collection at MIT.

"So what did you want to ask?" Luiz wore an orange snowsuit. His goggles rested on top of his forehead.

I stopped touching the meteorite. Red heat lamps were clamped to the top of the tent. Standing before the other scientists, I suddenly felt like the one about to be questioned. It was hard to breathe through the balaclava.

"What do you remember about him?"

Not much, it turned out. One scientist volunteered that he often ate alone; another said he never participated in group activities like evening card games and Ping-Pong. He sang in the shower on occasion, an American

song no one recognized. He had a stutter, though sometimes it was barely noticeable.

"What about the other times?" I asked.

"He could barely say his own name," Luiz said.

"How much longer was he supposed to stay with you?"
I wished I had a notepad. I would remember everything,
of course, but writing it down would have made me feel
official and organized, like I was asking questions that
might lead us somewhere.

"Two more weeks," Luiz said.

"And when did you last see him?"

There was silence, the shaking of heads. Someone
thought they saw him the morning of the explosion, pour-
ing a cup of coffee in the break room.

"Nothing else?" These weren't the questions I came
with, not really, but maybe if we kept talking a door would
open and I could ask something like *Did you know he had a
sister?* Or, *Did he seem happy?* Or, *What did he love about
being here?*

"I crawled out of the station." The words came from
the woman in a sharp burst. The hood of her parka was
down and auburn hair peeked through the top of her balaclava. Bianca, that was her name.

"On my stomach, through fire, smoke. This is what I
remember." She swept her hand toward the group. "No
one was thinking about your brother. We barely knew
him. We can't understand what you're doing here."

She pulled up her hood and walked out of the research

tent. The other three scientists looked at Luiz, who shrugged and said something in Spanish, before following her.

I watched them go. The tent flapped open, revealing a pale wedge of sky. Already I was failing as a detective.

"I didn't mean for it to go like that," I said.

"You want to know the truth?" Luiz said. "Your brother was a beaker."

"A what?"

"A beaker. A scientist who can't get along with the others. It wasn't a privilege for him to be at our station. They were tired of him at McMurdo."

At breakfast, Annabelle had bragged that she could teach me to say "asshole" in any language. If you spent enough time in Antarctica, you learned a little of everything.

"Ojete." I picked up a meteorite the size of a grape and threw it at his feet. "Ojete, ojete."

Luiz looked down at the rock, unfazed. I left the tent and walked away from the station. I tried to run but kept slipping on the ice. When I finally stopped and looked back, the U-shaped building was minuscule against the vastness of the land. It was like standing in the middle of a white sea—ice in all directions, stretching into infinity. I pulled at the balaclava. I wanted to take it off, but couldn't figure out how. The thought of venturing any farther was suddenly terrifying.

Annabelle had explained that most researchers came for short stints, a handful of weeks or months. Few stayed as long as a year, like my brother had. There was the feeling that nothing but the elements could touch you out here, and I understood that was something he would have appreciated. Since we had been close, I could make these kinds of calculations.

I turned in a circle, still looking. I imagined my brother trekking across the ice, fascinated by the world that existed beneath. My throat ached from the cold. It was impossible to distinguish land from sky.

It happened right after Eve's seventeenth birthday, in Concord, where she had grown up. She had been reading Jane Austen in a park and was just starting home. She remembered the soft yellow blanket rolled under her arm, the page she had dog-eared, the streaks of gold in the sky. She was on the edge of the park when she felt an arm wrap around her chest. For a moment, she thought someone was giving her a hug, a classmate or a cousin. She had lots of cousins in Concord. But then there was the knife at her throat and the gray sedan with the passenger door flung open. She dropped the Jane Austen and the blanket on the sidewalk. Somewhere, she imagined, those things were in a collection of crime scene photos.

At the Burren, she'd stopped there. Her martini glass was empty. The band was playing a Bruce Springsteen cover. She balled up her cocktail napkin and asked if I wanted to dance. She was wearing a silk turquoise dress and T-strap heels. Her bracelet shone on her wrist. She took my hand and we dipped and twirled. Men watched us. One even tried to cut in.

Two days later, I woke to the sound of my bedroom door opening. It was midnight. Eve stood in the doorway in a white nightgown. She got into bed with me and started telling me the rest, or most of the rest. She lay on her back. I watched her lips move in the darkness and wondered if my brother had noticed that his wife was no longer beside him. Soon he would be departing for a monthlong research trip to study the Juan de Fuca Plate in Vancouver, leaving us in each other's care.

The man was a stranger. He was fat around the middle. He had a brown beard and a straight white scar under his right eye. In the car, he tuned the radio to a sports station. He told her that if she did anything—scream, jump out—he would stab her in the heart. He drove them to a little house on a dirt road in Acton, where she stayed for three days.

Her parents had money. She told herself that he was just going to hold her for ransom; she didn't allow herself to consider that maybe he had other ideas. The thing she remembered most vividly from the car ride was the radio, the sound of a crowd cheering in a stadium.

"That and one of those green, tree-shaped things you hang from the rearview mirror," she said. "To freshen the air." This explained why she hated Christmas trees, why the scent alone made her light-headed and queasy. On our first holiday together, she'd told us she was allergic to pine and we'd gotten a plastic tree instead.

"How did you get away?" I asked.

"I didn't." She blinked. Her eyelashes were so pale, they were almost translucent. "I was rescued."

Eve had been half-right about the man's intentions. After holding her for forty-eight hours, he placed a ransom demand; it didn't take long for the authorities to figure out the rest. The police found her in a basement. Her wrists were tied to a radiator with twine. She was wearing a long white T-shirt with a pocket on the front. She had no idea where it had come from or what had happened to her clothes. Right before she was rescued, she remembered tracking the beam of a flashlight as it moved down the wall.

In the months that followed, the man's attorney had him diagnosed with a dissociative disorder, something Eve had never heard of before. He hadn't been himself when he had taken her, hadn't been himself in Acton. That was their claim. He got seven years and was out in five due to overcrowding. Her parents advised her to move on with her life. *He's been punished*, her father once said. *What else do you want to happen?* Now she just spoke to them on the phone every few months. They didn't even know she had gotten married.

"Where is he now?" I asked. "Do you know?"

"I've lost track of him." She tugged at the comforter. Her foot brushed against mine.

This was not a secret Eve had shared with my brother. I should have been thinking about him—how I couldn't believe he did not know about this, how he needed to know about this—but I wasn't. Instead I was trying to understand how anyone survived this world of head-on collisions and lunatic abductors and all the other things one had little hope of recovering from.

"I never went to therapy, but acting is having a therapeutic effect," she said next.

"How so?" During one of her epic phone conversations, I'd glimpsed her sprawled out on the living room sofa, painting her toenails and speaking in French. I'd picked up the landline in the kitchen, curious to know who she was talking to, but there had just been her voice and the buzz of the line. I'd wondered if it was some kind of acting exercise.

"Getting to disappear into different characters. Getting to not be myself."

I remembered her face on the stage in Medford. She was supposed to be Miranda, but her eyes had never stopped being Eve.

In time, I would learn it was possible to tell a secret, but also keep a piece of it close to yourself. That was what happened with Eve, who never told me what, exactly, went on during those three days in Acton. The floor was damp concrete. He fed her water with a soup spoon. I never got much more than that.

Of course, I could only assume the worst.

———

The aurora australis was Luiz's idea of a peace offering. We met in the observation room after dinner. It had been dark for hours. Despite my studies in astronomy, I couldn't get over how clear the sky was in Antarctica. I'd never seen so many stars, and it was comforting to feel close to something I had once loved. Annabelle and the others had gone back to work. I still hadn't forgiven Luiz for calling my brother a beaker.

"I've had too much ice time," he said. "I've gotten too used to the way this place can swallow people up." In his first month in Antarctica, two of his colleagues hiked to a subglacial lake and fell through the ice, into a cavern. By the time they were rescued, their bodies were eaten up with frostbite. One lost a hand; the other a leg.

"So it's Antarctica's fault you're an asshole?" I said.

"I blame everything on Antarctica," he said. "Just ask my ex-wife."

"Divorced!" I said. "What a surprise."

Luiz had arrived with two folded-up lounge chairs under his arms. They were made of white plastic, the kind of thing you'd expect to see at the beach. In the summer months, when there was no night, the scientists lounged on them in their snow pants and thermal shirts, a kind of Antarctic joke.

"I got them out of storage." He had arranged the chairs so they were side by side. "Just for you."

We reclined in our lounge chairs and stared through the glass. Since we were indoors, I was wearing my New Hampshire gear, the tassel hat and the leather gloves. A wisp of green light swirled above us.

"Tell me more about the explosion," I said, keeping my eyes on the sky.

The early word from the inspectors had confirmed his suspicions: a gas leak in the machine room. They were alleging questionable maintenance practices, because it was impossible to have a disaster without a cause. When the explosion happened, the three people working in the machine room were killed, along with two scientists in a nearby hallway. A researcher from Rio de Janeiro died from smoke inhalation; she and Bianca had worked together for years. Others were hospitalized with third- and fourth-degree burns. But my brother, he should have made it out. His seismograph was on the opposite end. He'd been sleeping next to it, on a foam mattress, for godsakes. Everyone thought he was crazy.

The green light returned, brighter this time. It was halo-shaped and hovering above the observation room. I hadn't stayed with astronomy long enough to see the auroras in anything other than photos and slides. I thought back to a course in extragalactic astronomy, to the lectures on Hubble's law and the quasars that radiated red light and the tidal pull of supermassive black holes, which terrified me. In college, I had imagined myself working in remote observatories and seeing something new in the sky.

"He thought he'd found an undiscovered fault line," Luiz continued. "He was compiling his data. No one believed him. The peninsula isn't known for seismic activity. He was the only one in that part of the building who didn't survive."

"Where were you during the explosion?" I watched the circle of light contract and expand.

"Outside. Scraping ice off our snow tractor."

So that was his guilt: he hadn't been close enough to believe he was going to die. He couldn't share in the trauma of having to save your own life, or the life of someone else; he could only report the facts. My brother had been too close, Luiz not close enough.

"We hadn't spoken in a long time." The halo dissolved and a sheet of luminous green spread across the horizon, at once beautiful and eerie.

"I asked him about family," Luiz said. "He didn't mention a sister."

I closed my eyes and thought about my brother in that hallway. I saw doorways alight with fire and black, curling smoke. His watch felt heavy on my wrist.

"Luiz," I said. "Do you have any secrets?"

"Too many to count." Silence fell over us in a way that made me think this was probably true. I pictured him tallying his secrets like coins. The sky hummed with green.

Later he explained the lights to me, the magnetic fields, the collision of electrons and atoms. I didn't tell him this was information I already knew. He reached for my hand

and pulled off one of my gloves. He placed it on his chest and put his hand over it.

I sat up and took the glove back from him. He held on to it for a moment, smiling, before he let go.

"Of course," Luiz said. "You are married."

That afternoon, I'd e-mailed my husband from the recreation room: *Still getting the lay of the land. Don't worry: polar bears are in the north pole.* He was a real estate agent and always honest about his properties—what needed renovating, if there were difficult neighbors. He believed the truth was as easy to grasp as an apple or a glass of water. That was why I had married him.

"Yes," I said. "But it doesn't have anything to do with that."

As it turned out, Eve had lied about losing track of the man who had taken her. After his release from prison, she had kept very careful track, aided by a cousin in Concord, a paralegal who had access to a private investigator. It was February when she came to me with news of him. We were sitting in a windowseat and drinking tea and looking out at the snow-covered lawn. A girl passed on the sidewalk, carrying ice skates and a pink helmet.

"He's in a hospital," she said. "Up on the Cape. He might not get out. Something to do with his lungs." She sighed with her whole body.

"And?" I said.

"And I want to see him."

"Oh, Eve. I think that's a terrible idea."

"Probably." She blew on her tea. "Probably it is."

In the weeks that followed, she kept at it. She talked about it while we folded laundry and swept the front steps. She talked about it when I met her for drinks after her rehearsals—she was an understudy for a production of *Buried Child* at the Repertory Theater—and while we rode the T, the train clacking over the tracks when we rose aboveground to cross the river. Eve explained that her parents had kept her from the court proceedings. She had wanted to visit him in prison, but that had been forbidden too. Now he was very sick. She was running out of chances.

"Chances for what?" We were waiting for the T in Central Square, on our way home from dinner. On the platform, a man was playing a violin for change. Eve had been in rehearsal earlier and was still wearing the false eyelashes and heavy red lipstick.

"To tell him that I made it." She raised her hands. Her gold bracelet slid down her wrist. "That I'm an actress. That I got married. That he wasn't the end of me. That I won."

"How about a phone call?" I said. "Or a letter?"

The T came through the tunnel and ground to a stop. The doors opened. People spilled onto the platform. A woman carrying a sleeping child slipped between me and Eve. My brother had been in Vancouver for two weeks and called home on Sunday mornings.

"You don't understand," she said as we boarded the train. "It has to be done in person."

I missed the perfect chance to tell my brother everything. The day before he left for Vancouver, I went to see him at MIT. His department was housed in the Green Building. From the outside, you could see a white radome on the roof. The basement level was connected to the MIT tunnel system. The first time I visited him on campus, he told me you could take the tunnels all the way to Kendall Square.

"How about some air?" I said after I found him hunched over a microscope, surrounded by open laptops and notebooks and empty coffee mugs. The lenses of his glasses were smudged. Eve had been trimming his hair and there was an unevenness to the cut that made him look like he was holding his head at a funny angle. He was surprised to see me. I hadn't told him I was coming.

We left campus and walked along Memorial Drive. By the river it was cold and windy. We pulled up our coat collars and tightened our scarves. We turned onto the Longfellow Bridge and kept going until we were standing between two stone piers with tiny windows. They reminded me of medieval lookout towers. We gazed out at the river and the city skyline beyond it.

I should have had a plan, but I didn't. Rather, the

weight of Eve's secret had propelled me toward him, the way I imagined a current tugs at the objects that find their way into its waters.

"The house," my brother said. "Is everything okay there?"

Without him realizing, he had become an anchor for me and Eve; we always knew he was there, in the background. With his departure, I could feel a shift looming: subtle as a change in the energy, the way air cools before a storm. But this was before Eve had brought up going to the Cape. I didn't know how to explain what I was feeling, or if I should even try. I couldn't imagine what the right words would be.

"Everything's fine."

"Eve says you've been like a sister," he said.

"We'll miss you," I said. "Don't forget to call."

A gust nearly carried away my hat. I pulled it down over my ears. Snow clouds were settling over brownstones and high-rises. My brother put his arm around me and started talking about the Juan de Fuca Plate, his voice bright with excitement. I could detect only the slightest trace of a stutter. The plate was bursting with seismic activity, a hotbed of shifts and tremors. I wrapped my arms around his waist and leaned into him. With his free hand, he drew the different kinds of fault lines—listric, ring, strike-slip—in the air.

———

The near-constant darkness of Antarctica made my body confused about when to rest. At three in the morning, I got out of bed and pulled fleece-lined boots over my flannel pajamas. I put on my gloves and hat. Annabelle was babbling in Spanish. At dinner, under the fluorescent lights of the mess hall, I'd noticed a scattering of freckles on her cheekbones and thought of Eve. I had to stop myself from reaching across the table and touching her face.

The station was quiet. The doorways were dark and shuttered. I peered through shadows at the end of hallways and around corners like I was searching for something in particular—what that would be, I didn't know. I drifted to the front of the station. In the mudroom, I surveyed the red windbreakers hanging on the wall, the bundles of goggles and gloves, the rows of boots. The entrance was a large steel door with a porthole window. I thought about opening the door, just for a moment, even though the temperature outside would be deep in the negatives. I imagined my hair turning into icicles, my eyes to glass.

Through the window, the station lights illuminated the outbuildings and the ice. The darkness was too thick, too absolute, to see anything more. When Luiz first told me that the rescue crew hadn't found any remains, there had been a moment when I'd thought my brother hadn't died in the explosion at all. Maybe he hadn't even been in the building. Maybe he had seen smoke rising from the station and realized this was his chance to vanish. I could picture him boarding an icebreaker and sailing to Uruguay or Cape

Town. Standing on the deck of a ship and watching a new horizon emerge.

For a long time, I kept watch through the window, willing myself to see a figure surface from the night. Who was to say he hadn't sailed to another land? Who was to say he wasn't somewhere in that darkness? For him, I would open the door. For him, I would endure the cold. But, of course, nothing was out there.

In the observation room, after the aurora australis had left the sky, I'd turned to Luiz and said: *Here's what I want.* The idea had come suddenly and with force. I wanted to go to the Brazilian station, to the site of the explosion. At first, Luiz said it was impossible; it would involve chartering a helicopter, for one thing. I told him that if he could figure out a way to make this happen, I'd stop asking questions and get on the next flight to New Zealand, the first step in my journey home. I didn't care how much the helicopter ride cost. He promised to see what he could do.

I left the window and slipped back into the hallway. A light was still on in the recreation room. I sat in the armchair next to the phone. I'd tucked my calling card into my pajama pocket, thinking I might phone my husband. Instead I dialed the number of the house in Davis Square, which I still knew by heart. The phone rang five times before someone answered. I'd thought a machine might come on and I could leave whoever lived there now a message about polar bears and green lights in the sky. For a moment, I imagined my sister-in-law picking up. *Où avez-vous été?* she would say. *Where have you been?*

A woman answered. Her voice was high and uncertain, not at all like Eve's. I pressed the phone against my ear. I pulled on the cord and thought about fault lines. I could see a dark streak running down my ribs, a fissure in my sternum.

"Hello?" she said. Static flared on the line. "How can I help you?"

It was a military hospital, just outside Barnstable. The morning we left, Eve talked to my brother on the phone and said we were going to see the glass museum in Sandwich. I drove. She was dressed in jeans and a gray sweatshirt, unadorned by jewelry, the plainest I'd ever seen her. She rested her socked feet on the dashboard and told me what her cousin had discovered about this man. He'd been in the military, dishonorably discharged. Years ago he'd been involved with a real estate scam involving fraudulent mortgages, but pleaded out of jail time. He had two restraining orders in his file.

"I'm surprised someone hasn't killed him already." She cracked the window. The air was heavy with moisture and salt.

We drove through Plymouth and Sandwich. From the highway, I saw a billboard ad for the glass museum. At the hospital—a labyrinthine gray building just off the highway—we learned he was in the ICU. We pretended to be family.

He was in a room with two other men. A thin curtain hung between each of the beds. Eve slowly walked from one to another. The first patient was gazing at the TV bolted to the wall. The second was drinking orange juice from a straw. The third was asleep. He wore a white hospital gown. His gray hair was shorn close to the scalp. One hand rested on his stomach, the other on the mattress. I followed Eve to his bedside. His face was speckled with broken capillaries, his cheekbones sharp, his slender forearms bruised. He was on oxygen and attached to a heart monitor. I smelled something sour.

"Are you sure this is him?" I asked Eve, even though I could see the scar. It was just as she had described: a thin white line under his eye.

"Don't say it." She walked over to the window and looked out at the parking lot.

"Say what?"

"That's he's old and frail and defenseless." Eve turned from the window. "He's not like that at all. Not on the inside."

She slumped down on the linoleum floor. A nurse was attending to the patient next to us. I watched her shadow through the curtain. She carried away a tray with an empty glass on it. She told the man who had been drinking the juice to have a nice day.

"So what do we do now?" I asked. "Wake him up?"

"I'm thinking," Eve said. "I'm thinking of what to do."

It took her a long time to do her thinking. I listened to the din of the TV. I thought a game show was on from the way people kept calling out numbers.

Finally, Eve jumped up and started digging through her purse. She took out a tube of lipstick, the garish red color she wore onstage, and raised it like a prize.

"Okay," she said. "I have my first idea."

She uncapped the lipstick and went to the sleeping man. She smeared color across his mouth. I stood on the other side of his bed and stared down, trying to see the evil in him. Eve used the lipstick to rouge his cheeks before passing it to me. I drew red half-circles above his eyebrows. We waited for him to wake up, to cry for help, but he only made a faint gurgling sound. His hand twitched on his stomach. That was all.

"Now I have another idea," Eve said.

For this second thing, she wanted to be alone. I looked at the clown's face we had given this man. My stomach felt strange. On the intercom, a doctor was being paged to surgery.

"Five minutes. Three hundred seconds." Her face was free of makeup, her freckles visible. She'd had her teeth bleached recently and they looked abnormally bright. "That's all I'm asking for, Lee."

After what had happened to her, wasn't she owed five minutes alone with him? That was my thinking at the time. On my way out of the ICU, the same nurse who picked up the juice glass asked if I'd had a pleasant visit.

I waited on the sidewalk. I watched people come and go through the automatic doors. An old man on crutches. A woman in a wheelchair. A nurse in lavender scrubs. What was the worst thing these people had done?

Eve stayed in the hospital for fifty-seven minutes. I couldn't bring myself to go back inside. I paced in the cold. I had forgotten my gloves and my hands went numb. Even though I'd never smoked in my life, I asked a doctor smoking outside if I could bum a cigarette.

"These things will kill you." The doctor winked and flipped open his pack.

When Eve emerged from the hospital, she took my hand and pulled me toward the car. We drove in silence. She rested her head against the window. When I tried to turn on the radio, she touched my wrist. Her fingertips were waxy with lipstick.

"Please," she said.

After a half hour on the road, I exited at Sagamore Beach. The silence felt like a pair of hands around my throat. Eve didn't object when I parked in the designated beach lot, empty on account of it being February, or when we climbed over dunes and through sea grass. Cold sand leaked into our shoes. I didn't stop until I reached water.

We stood on the edge of Cape Cod Bay. The water was still and gray. Clusters of rock extended into the bay like fingers. A white mist hung over us. A freighter was visible in the distance.

"Why didn't you come out when you said you would?" The freighter was moving farther away. When it vanished from sight, it looked like it had gone into a cloud. "What were you doing in there?"

"We were talking." Her face was dewy from the mist. Her pale hair had frizzed. She picked up a white stone and threw it into the water.

"So he woke up?"

"Yes," she said. "He did and then he didn't."

She picked up another stone. It was gray with a black dot in the center. She held on to it for a little while, turning it over in her hands, before it went into the bay.

In Cambridge, she wanted to be dropped at the Repertory Theater. She had to tell the director that she couldn't make rehearsal; she promised to come home soon. Her hair was still curled from being at the beach. Her cheeks and forehead were damp. I tried to determine if anything had shifted in her eyes.

I idled on Brattle Street until Eve had gone into the theater. Her purse swung from her shoulder and somewhere inside it was that lipstick. I kept telling myself that the most dangerous part was over. We were home now. Everything would be the same as before.

But no. Nothing would be the same as before. Eve never talked to her director. She never returned to the house. I had to call my brother and tell him to come home from Vancouver. When I picked him up at the airport, it was late. I waited in baggage claim. Long before he noticed me, I spotted him coming down the escalator, a duffel bag slung over his shoulder. He had lost weight. His hair had grown out. I remembered thinking that I wished we'd taken the time to learn how to talk to each other. When he finally saw me, he tried to call out *Lee*, but his stutter was as bad as it had been in childhood. It took him three tries to say my name.

A report was filed. Eve's parents—a frail, bookish couple—came into town from Concord. An investigation went on for weeks. There was no sign of Eve, no sign of foul play. As gently as he could, the detective asked us to consider the possibility that she had run away. Apparently women—young mothers, young wives—did this more frequently than people might think. I told everyone I'd dropped Eve at the theater, but the truth stopped there. Every time I tried to say more, I felt like a stone was lodged in my throat.

My brother knew I was holding something back. He pressed me for information. Had she been taking an inordinate amount of calls? Had anything peculiar arrived in the mail? Was she having an affair with a cast mate? Had we really gone to the glass museum in Sandwich? I submitted to these questions, even though I didn't—couldn't, I felt at the time—always tell the truth. And I knew he was confronting his own failing, the fact that he hadn't cared to know any of this until after his wife was gone.

We waited months before we packed up her belongings: the silk dresses, the shoes, the jewelry, the plays. Her possessions had always seemed abundant, but only filled three cardboard boxes. My brother kept them stacked at the foot of his bed. When he moved, two boxes went to Eve's parents and he took the other one with him. I don't know what happened to her things after that.

The last time he asked me a question about Eve, we were on the front porch. It was late spring. The trees were blooming green and white. I was in a rocking chair. My brother was leaning against the porch railing, facing the street.

"Do you think you knew her better than I did?" he said.

"No." Once I had come upon them in the upstairs hallway: they were pressed against the wall, kissing, and he was twisting one of Eve's wrists behind her back. It was clear that the pleasure was mutual, which led me to believe that she might enjoy a degree of pain. Only my brother could say how much.

He stared out at the glowing streetlights. I could tell from the way he licked his lips and squeezed the railing that he did not believe me.

By summer, we had moved into separate apartments: his in Beacon Hill, so he could be closer to MIT; mine in the North End, scrunched between a pastry shop and a butcher. I bounced from one entry-level lab job to another, my ambition dulled, while I watched my brother pull his own disappearing act: into his dissertation; into the conference circuit; into one far-flung expedition after another.

The Philippines, Australia, Haiti. Antarctica. The phone calls and postcards turned from weekly to monthly to hardly at all.

I got married the year I turned thirty. My brother came, but left before the cake was served. It was too painful, watching the night unfold; I understood this without him ever saying so. I told my husband that he had been married briefly and, years ago, we'd all lived together in Davis Square. Soon I had a child. I worked part-time as a lab assistant, sorting someone else's data, and cared for him, which was not the life I'd imagined for myself, but it seemed like a fair exchange: I hadn't kept sufficient watch over Eve, hadn't kept her from danger. This was my chance to make it up. I tried to tell myself she was someplace far away and happy. I tried to forget that she might have been in trouble, that she might have needed us. When I looked at my son, I tried not to think about all the things I could never tell him. I tried to shake the feeling that I was living someone else's life.

In the years to come, I would start so many letters to my brother, each one beginning in a different way: *Eve was not who you thought* and *I don't know how it all started* and *How could you not have known?* I never got very far, because I knew I was still lying. The letter I finally finished— addressed to McMurdo Station but never mailed—opened with: *None of this was your fault.*

Another thing I never told him: before leaving the house in Davis Square, I cut open one of Eve's boxes and found her gold bracelet in a tiny plastic bag. The chain was tarnished. I popped open the locket. The frames were empty. I took the bracelet and resealed the box with packing tape. I held on to it—never wearing it, always hiding it away, even before there were people to hide it from. My husband found it once, and I said it had been a gift from my mother. I imagined other people discovering the bracelet through the years and me telling each one a different story. I carried it with me to Antarctica, tucked in the side pocket of my suitcase, though I was never able to bring it out into the open.

Not long after Eve's disappearance, I looked up the name of her abductor on a computer: Randall Smith. I'd heard her say it aloud only once, in the hospital. After a little searching, I found an obituary. He had died the day after our visit, survived by no one. The obituary said it was natural causes, which explained nothing.

It was twilight when we flew over Admiralty Bay. Luiz said that if I watched the water carefully, I might see leopard seals. The pilot was from the Netherlands, hired for a price that would horrify my husband when the check posted. Luiz's boss had gotten wind of our expedition and wasn't at all pleased; that morning, he'd called from Brazil and told Luiz that he was not in the business of escorting tourists. Soon I would have to get on the plane to New Zealand, like I had promised, but I wasn't completely out of time.

The landscape was different on the peninsula. The ice was sparser, exposing the rocky peaks of mountains and patches of black soil near the coastline. When the explosion site came into view, it looked like a dark scar on the snow.

The helicopter touched down. Black headsets swallowed our ears, muffling the sound of the propellers. The helicopter swayed as it landed. I could feel the engine rumbling beneath us; it made my skin vibrate inside my many layers of clothes. Luiz got out first, then helped me onto the ice. The pilot shouted something in Dutch, which Luiz translated: soon the twilight would be gone; he didn't want to fly back in the dark.

Together we approached the wreckage. Luiz still had his headset on. I had taken mine off too soon and now my ears buzzed. Up close, the site was smaller than I'd expected: a black rectangle the size of the swimming pool I took my son to in the summer. Nothing of the structure remained except for metal beams jutting from ridges of ash and debris. The sky was a golden haze.

"I told you there wasn't much to see." He slipped off his headset. His face was covered except for his eyes. I was wearing a balaclava too and knew I looked the same.

"Tell me what it was like before."

The station had been shaped like a horseshoe. He

pointed to the empty spaces where the mess hall used to be, the dormitory, the bathroom, my brother's seismograph. Their base had been smaller than Belgrano. They didn't have an observation room or heated research tents. Everything had been contained beneath one roof.

I stepped in the ash and listened to it crunch under my boots. I passed black spears of wood and warped beams. One section of the site was even more charred, the ground scooped in. I stood inside the depression and looked at the bits of glinting metal. I picked up something the size of a quarter. I wasn't sure what it had been before; the fire had made it glossy and flat. I slipped it into my pocket and kept walking. I told myself it was evidence; I just didn't know what kind.

The wind blew flurries of ash around my legs. On the other end of the site, I looked for some sign of my brother's seismograph. I came across a spoon, the handle melted into a glob of metal, and a lighter. I put those things in my pocket too. More evidence. Luiz was still on the edge of the site. By then I understood he was someone who had no desire to go searching for things. He didn't even collect the meteorites; that was left to his team. His only concern was classifying them. The helicopter would be ready for us soon, but the sky still held a dull glow.

There were so many times when I wanted to tell my brother everything, when, in the middle of the night, I wanted to kneel by his bed and whisper, *I have a secret*. In Cambridge, I'd told myself these were Eve's secrets to keep or expose; it was her life to walk away from, if that's what she wanted. The more time that passed, the more unimaginable the truth seemed. To admit one lie would mean admitting another and then another.

I imagined myself at home in New Hampshire, arranging everything on the living room floor. A map of Antarctica, with stars to mark the bases: McMurdo; here; Belgrano. My brother's watch. Eve's empty locket. The photo he mailed, without a note, when he first arrived in Antarctica. He was wearing a yellow snowsuit and standing outside McMurdo, surrounded by bright white ice. Around these materials, I would place the metals I had collected at the site and try to see something: a pattern, a sign. Or maybe I would just read aloud the last letter I wrote to him. Or maybe, in the helicopter, I would turn to Luiz and tell him everything.

The sky was almost dark. I was back inside the depression. I was sitting down in it and hugging my knees. I had no memory of walking over there and stepping into the hole; I had just done it automatically. Luiz was calling to me. The wind carried his voice away.

*Maybe it was just an iguana*, I heard my brother say.

In Antarctica, I did not know if he had denied himself the chance to get out of the burning building. I did not know what he believed I knew, or what would have changed if I'd given him the truth. I did not know if I would ever see Eve again. I did not know what had happened in that hospital room, or in Acton. I thought about the grief of wanting to know what was not knowable, the grief my brother must have carried, a different pain than my own.

I did not know certain things because I had chosen to turn away from the knowledge. In Antarctica, I decided that was the worst thing I'd ever done, that refusal.

The stars were coming out. Luiz was crossing the site, waving and calling my name. The temperature was dropping. My eyes watered. I sank deeper into the hole.

In Antarctica, I did not know that a month after I left, Luiz would became trapped in a whiteout and lose two fingers to frostbite. I did not know that the tibia would turn out to have belonged to my brother, that it would be shipped back to America in a metal box. I did not know if one day I would disappear and no one except a missing woman and a dead man would be able to tell the people who loved me why.

# THE GREATEST ESCAPE

My father leaving was his last act of magic. He had locked himself in a glass aquarium filled with water. The idea was to disappear from the aquarium and reappear onstage. At the time, my mother was pregnant with me. She saw what happened at the rehearsal, saw it with her own eyes: he vanished but never returned. No one could explain it. It was supposed to have been an illusion, after all. The stage was searched. Even the real police looked for him, but he was gone. *Gone where?* I asked her, and she said nobody knew, not even the world's greatest magicians. She once told me there was a cruelty to magic because it takes a thing, transforms it, and then turns it back into what it was. My father had forgotten the turning-back part.

That wasn't the only story my mother told me. In 1910, Harry Houdini escaped from a straitjacket while suspended from a crane. Two years later, he freed himself from a nailed-shut packing crate that had been dropped into the

East River. That was the kind of magic I dreamed about. I wanted us to make each other levitate and disappear, to perform in Las Vegas and Times Square. And where was I instead? Standing beneath the red lights of a dinner theater stage in Hollywood, Florida, watching my mother balance a globe of fire in her hand.

Of course, the fire wasn't real. It was a Level 1 illusion, the best she could manage these days, despite having trained at a world-famous magic school in the real Hollywood, out in California. At the school, she had been working her way to Level 3, which was the Houdini stuff—the harrowing escapes, the ability to manipulate reality and time. She claimed her skills had weakened when my father disappeared, and left her almost entirely after I was born.

My parents had met at magic school. In their first class, my father could make a cockatoo vanish from its cage better than anyone. He became the headmaster's protégé. His stage name was the Great Heraldo. Once I looked up the school online, in the dinner theater owner's office. The building resembled a castle, with a stone wall and spires. In the photos, the windows glowed with gold light. I spent a long time staring at them and wondering what was happening inside.

After my father disappeared, my mother needed a change of scenery. She'd thought Hollywood, Florida, might be better than the one in California, but here it was swampy and flat and there were hurricanes instead of earthquakes and fires. I'd been part of her act since child-hood. We used to have more families in the audience, but now the men who wandered over from nearby hotels and drank during the shows were the only ones who came to watch. According to the owner, there was stiffer competi-tion from new venues in Fort Lauderdale and Boca Raton. He was a slight, stooped man with a thin black mustache, and he'd been pleading with my mother to shake things up. As I watched her hold the fire, the peaked orange flames stretching upward, like a plant toward light, I hoped she was capable of a greater kind of magic. That she still had it in her.

As the assistant, I was dressed in a gold bathing suit and red high heels. My mother wore a black pantsuit with a bow tie and a top hat. Her cape billowed behind her when she moved. She said a real magician would never be caught dead in a bathing suit, but I was seventeen and capable of handling indignity. After the fire trick, she made a quar-ter vanish and reappear from my cleavage. I liked having her close to me onstage. I could see the mascara crusted on her eyelashes and smell the gel that kept her blond hair shellacked under her hat. When I noticed her lips crack-ing beneath her red lipstick, I knew she wasn't drinking enough water. When her pupils looked swollen, I knew she wasn't getting enough sleep. When one man starting chanting *Kiss!* and my mother threw out a smile—fast, wide, full of teeth—I knew she was wishing him terrible things.

For the grand finale, I disappeared. My mother opened a trapdoor in the center of the stage. I waved to the audience before crawling inside. She closed the door and said *Shazam!*—my cue to crawl into the compartment under the stage. The space was the size of a dumbwaiter and smelled like cedar. I sat with my knees pulled to my chest, so I didn't get splinters in my legs. I listened to the trapdoor open and a volunteer lumber onto the stage to inspect the empty space. Before shows, my mother always dusted me with glitter, which left behind a fine gold grit. My skin felt like it was coated in sand.

When she opened the trapdoor a second time, I popped up like a jack-in-the-box. The audience applauded half-heartedly. I curtsied. My mother took a bow. The heat had made her foundation run. Under the lights, it looked like her skin was melting. A black velvet curtain swung closed in front of us.

At the bar, men were lining up to buy me drinks. I didn't care what they were—a beer, a warm glass of white wine, a whiskey sour. Each one made me feel like I was being carried away on a cloud. Before long, one of the men would manage to clear away the rest, the one who bought the most drinks, who told the most jokes. My name was Crystal, but sometimes they pronounced it "Cristal," like the champagne.

Tonight it was a man in a wrinkled suit with a thick gold band on his left ring finger. He had a fleshy jawline, little blue eyes, and big ears. A soft, decent face. He was in Hollywood on business, staying at a hotel down the street. He had once seen Penn and Teller perform in New York City. In their act, one magician fired a gun and the other caught the bullet in his mouth.

"Can you imagine such a thing?" he said. "How much one would have to trust the other?"

I could not.

He was buying my third martini. At the theater, martinis were served in a clear plastic cup with a trio of tiny green olives, the smallest I'd ever seen. I wore a pink silk bathrobe over my bathing suit, the sash tied in a loose bow. I teetered in my heels. My mouth was slick with vodka and raspberry-flavored lip gloss.

"Do a trick!" The man clutched my martini with his fat, damp hands. This kind of exchange, a little pro bono magic, was always expected. "Won't you please do a trick?"

I gave him the same smile my mother had flashed her audience—full of teeth and menace—and pulled a blue flower from behind my ear, the first trick she ever taught me. I tucked the flower into his shirt pocket. He handed me the drink. I swallowed the olives whole.

Tea candles flickered on the bar. Ricky, the bartender, was rinsing out beer glasses. I knew my mother was still backstage, in our dressing room. She had an elaborate postshow routine: skin care, hair care, special stretching exercises. I could see her wiping away her lipstick and dreaming of a different life. Where was the magic for that?

I let the man stroke my neck. He rested a hand on my waist. I didn't know his name, but in my mind I had started calling him Bill. Poor Bill. Didn't he know that you should never trust a half-naked girl in a bar at this hour of the night?

Bill asked where else I could make flowers appear from. I fluttered my eyelashes. I leaned forward and slipped my hand inside his pocket. He sighed dreamily. I pulled out his wallet, rolled it up my arm, and slipped it into the back of my bathing suit. This was a variation on another trick my mother had taught me, where I vanished a wand by covering it with a handkerchief and sliding it up my sleeve. In the morning, Bill might call the theater and ask Ricky—I threw him a little cash for his silence—about the wallet. But probably Bill's memory would be too foggy to remember where he'd been or who he'd been with. And even if it wasn't, he might be a little embarrassed that he'd spent his night pawing a teenager in a bathing suit. He was married. He probably had a mortgage and kids. He wouldn't want to make trouble.

I leaned in again and told Bill that I needed to freshen up. I kissed his cheek. Why not do him that one small kindness? When I pulled away, he was smiling a sick, stupid smile. Over his shoulder, I caught Ricky rolling his eyes as he wiped down the bar.

Of course, I never went back. Instead I found my mother sitting at the dressing table mirror and removing her makeup with cotton balls soaked in witch hazel. The table had uneven legs and cracked green paint. The oval mirror was fringed with rust. A small chandelier hung from the ceiling, but all the bulbs were missing.

It was July. In a month, I'd be back in school. My classmates were talking about college, but maybe I would go to Hollywood and study magic instead. I would ace my classes in divining and dematerialization. I would become the headmaster's pet. *Brava, Crystal!* he would say. *Brava!* Only I wouldn't fall in love or get pregnant or disappear or let my powers fade away.

I curled up on the chaise lounge my mother insisted on keeping even though it had moths. Bill's wallet held seventy dollars in cash, a chewing gum wrapper, and a Polaroid photo of a palm tree. No credit cards, no driver's license. For the last six months, I'd been saving up. I kept my money in a shoe box from Wholesale Magic. Something had shifted when I turned seventeen; I started to feel like I needed to make my own plans. I kept changing the location of the box—bottom dresser drawer, top closet shelf, under my bed—but that wasn't enough to prevent my mother from dipping into my supply.

"We should get a rabbit," she said, out of nowhere. She moved the cotton ball in circles across her face. She had high cheekbones and a long, elegant neck. Mascara had clotted in the corners of her eyes.

"I thought rabbit tricks were low-rent." I fanned myself with Bill's photo.

"Well, Crystal, clearly we'd have to do something out of the ordinary." She rubbed her palm with the cotton ball. The powder that made the fake fire always left a dark ring on her skin. I remembered that Houdini had called fire the most terrible of the elements. He also said his greatest escape was leaving Appleton, Wisconsin.

"Like what?"

My mother told me about a magic-school classmate who trained a rabbit to climb an invisible thread; from the audience, it looked like the animal was levitating. Another time, she had seen a magician place a rabbit on a tabletop, vanish it, and then make it reappear underneath the table.

I pointed out that what she was describing would require expensive new equipment and months of careful rabbit-training, which neither of us knew how to do.

"A nice rabbit," she continued. "Fat and white." She picked up the tiny toothbrush she used to exfoliate her lips.

In 1898, Ching Ling Foo conjured a small child from a bowl of water. For his Garden of Flowers trick, Harry Blackstone, Jr., made flowers multiply until the stage was brilliant with color. Was it possible to become famous, or even fill our dinky theater, with a rabbit? I didn't think so.

"This is the kind of magic that's going to put bodies in seats," she insisted. *Bodies in seats* was the owner's motto. "Only psychopaths dislike rabbits."

The last time my mother was this excited about a new trick, she ordered a five-hundred-dollar guillotine from a catalogue. Naturally, I was the one in the stocks. It should have been a dramatic illusion onstage. Even though I knew it was designed for magic, I would still get nervous waiting for the blade to drop. But my mother didn't perform the trick very well. She didn't talk about the history of the guillotine or place a bucket underneath my head or lead the audience in a countdown. And where was the guillotine now? Collecting dust backstage.

My mother dabbed white cream under her eyes. I examined the photo of the palm tree and wondered why someone would carry around such a thing. Over the months, I'd discovered some strange items in these wallets. One had five bucks and a surgical glove dusted in baby powder. Another held a postcard of people dressed in lobster costumes.

"Is it ever this hot in California?" I asked. We didn't have air-conditioning in the dressing room. My legs were sticking together.

"It's a different kind of heat." She pulled off the fake diamond studs she wore during shows and placed them on the table. "Did you know your father could predict when an earthquake was coming? He'd feel a trembling in his mouth." She tapped her bottom lip.

I looked again at Bill's photo and wondered if it could have been taken in California.

My mother spritzed perfume on her throat, then rose

from the table and flicked off the lights. This was the part of the night she hated the most: the show was over, the costumes peeled away, the makeup removed. Now there was nothing to do but slink upstairs, to our cramped apartment with the dusty window units and the temperamental stove. *Put bodies in seats, if you want new appliances*, the theater owner had told us. The apartment was cluttered with supplies: a Bible that sprouted flames, a silk rose that bloomed into a bouquet, collapsible wands. All around us was the promise of magic. I knew my mother would sit in the dark of her bedroom and have a drink. What she didn't know was that Ricky had slipped me a mini-bottle before I left, so I would be having one with her too.

In the morning, I woke feeling gummy with glitter and sweat. My window unit was blowing lukewarm air. A poster of the real Hollywood, an image of a white sign nestled in green hills, fluttered on the wall. I got up and wandered into the kitchen, where I found my mother standing by the sink, holding a white rabbit. I'd fallen asleep in my bathing suit and bathrobe. My feet were sore from the heels. I scratched my arm. The glitter was always giving me rashes. In my dreams, she had conjured the rabbit from nothing; in my dreams, we had an endless supply of talent and hope.

"I got him at PetSmart." She bounced the rabbit in her

arms. He had a sleek white coat and quick, red eyes. She had named him Merlin.

"With my money?" In the corner, there was a defunct saw-a-lady-in-half kit covered with a white sheet. Next to it, my mother had set up a large metal cage. The bottom was covered with wood chips. She had even gotten little blue dishes for water and rabbit pellets. A hundred dollars, at least.

"I'm the talent," she said. "It was never your money."

I went to my room and checked the shoe box, smoothing the crinkled bills as I counted. I was missing three fifties. I pushed the box back under my bed, wondering if there was such a thing as a place that would be safe from my mother.

Before our next show, she wanted to teach Merlin the levitating rabbit trick. The first step was training him to balance on his hind legs. We began that evening. By then I had showered and put on regular clothes. My mother was wearing a pink tracksuit. Her hair was in rollers. She was not looking especially magical. She placed Merlin on the kitchen floor. The air inside the apartment was heavy and still. The wall clock had been stuck at noon for a week.

She lifted her hand over the rabbit. Merlin looked toward the S-shaped crack in the ceiling. He seemed to be paying attention.

"Up," she said.

He pricked his ears. For a moment, I thought he was going to meet her hand, a miraculously trainable rabbit, but instead he bolted across the room and tried to shimmy under the stove.

"As I suspected," she said. "We'll need lots of practice."

We went on like this for hours: my mother commanding, Merlin finding new ways to flee. She'd already told the theater owner that we would be unveiling the rabbit in our next performance, which was three days away. I wished my father was here; I felt certain he would have trained Merlin in no time at all.

"Up," she said for what felt like the hundredth time, looming over the rabbit, her voice baritone. It was dark out. He rolled over on his side, as though we were putting him to sleep.

"Sleeping rabbit," I said. "That's a pretty lousy trick."

"Negativity is not a training tool, Crystal." She got a Dr Pepper from the fridge and ran the can across her forehead. I stroked Merlin's belly and felt the thumping of his heart.

My mother started telling me about when she and my father were living together in California, in an apartment in Toluca Lake. He would hypnotize her and get her to do all kinds of things. He would take photos and show them to her as proof: handstands until her face was purple, squeezing mustard into a bowl and eating it with a spoon, stripping naked and numbing her body with ice cubes. The image of my mother naked made me uneasy. I wondered where that photo was now. I imagined finding it in a wallet, what I would think.

"Maybe we could hypnotize Merlin." I pictured a hypnotized rabbit waltzing across the stage, or peeling a banana with his paws. That would be something to see.

I could tell my mother wasn't listening. She was kneeling on the floor and petting the rabbit's neck, which was glossy and rolled with fat.

"One day," she said. "One day I'll tell you things about him that you would not believe."

We practiced for two days without success. Merlin was always darting into the bathroom, where he would hide behind the toilet, leaving a trail of wood chips in his wake. Sometimes I pretended to not be able to find him even though I knew exactly where he was.

With our next performance upon us, my mother settled for the usual rabbit-in-a-hat trick. She brought out her stovepipe hat with the false bottom. We just had to train Merlin to sit inside, underneath a circle of black cardboard. Onstage, my mother would show the hat was empty by tilting it toward the audience, then cover it with a handkerchief and say *Shazam!* Afterward, she would push past the false bottom and pull out the rabbit. Amateur magic. If her classmates from magic school could see her now, they would be ashamed.

One evening, she sent me to the Sizzler for baby carrots. She had decided Merlin needed more positive reinforcement. I brought along a black briefcase, which looked ordinary enough, but opened in two places. In a performance, the briefcase was shown to be empty and then, from the hidden opening, the magician lifted out all manner of things: a baseball, a vase, a hammer. After the Sizzler, my next stop was Coco Cabana, the twenty-four-hour liquor store, where I planned to pinch mini-bottles from the shelves.

The store was owned by Mr. Phillips. He was always engrossed in a paper and never kept his minis behind the counter, the way other liquor stores did. I used to hang around long enough for him to tell me about what he was reading. He didn't seem to notice the way I now went straight to the back and left without buying anything. He would just say it was a shame that I didn't have time for stories. His son was a different matter. If he was around, he'd stand in the aisle and watch as I disappeared behind a shelf. Once he demanded I open the briefcase and I was pleased with myself for showing the empty side with a smile and a magician's flourish. I hoped he didn't inherit the store anytime soon.

"Hey, Crystal," Mr. Phillips called on my way out.

I waved but didn't stop. Four little vodkas were rattling around in the briefcase.

He shook a copy of the *Hollywood Gazette*. "Have I got a story for you."

I walked home on Surf Road, past palm trees like the one in Bill's photo and a long stretch of beach. The tide was coming in; dusk was settling over white villas and the peaks of distant high-rises. My hair was damp. I tasted salt on my upper lip. I drank two mini-bottles and tossed the empties into the recycling bin stationed outside a mint-green bungalow. Once, when I was young, my mother and I had passed a street magician on this very strip. He was making plastic balls disappear up his coat sleeves. I had tugged her hand and asked if he could be my father, and she'd laughed and said he wasn't even close to the kind of magician my father had been, to the Great Heraldo.

Outside the dinner theater, a man was hanging around the entrance. I didn't think he was waiting for me—no one was ever waiting for me—but before I could slip inside, he stepped into my path.

"I want my wallet back," he said.

It was Bill, wearing black pants and a dress shirt, the armpits ringed with sweat. He turned his wedding band on his finger. I was holding the package of baby carrots in one hand and the briefcase in the other.

"I bet the owner of this place would like to know what you've been up to," Bill said. "I bet he'd find it all very interesting."

The carrots were cold. I pressed the package against my forehead like a compress. Bill touched my elbow, a little roughly. He asked if I was paying attention.

"You're too late," I said. "Everything's gone."

"Even the photo?" He squinted at me. His cheeks and forehead shone.

It wouldn't have cost me anything to give the photo

back to him, but that would be hard evidence that I had stolen and that was bad for business. I had to look out for myself in practical ways. I couldn't rely on magic.

"I get it," I said. "You don't want your wife to find out you're a sleaze. Do you know how old I am? No? I'm a minor, for your information, and I bet some people would be very interested to know about that."

Bill took a step back. His face went slack, as though I had just slapped him. He didn't stop me when I opened the door and went inside.

The first time I went to Coco Cabana, I was fifteen. The night had brought a particularly bad show: we were still doing the saw-a-lady-in-half trick, and my mother had fumbled the reassembly. I was scrunched inside a wood box on wheels, which should have been reconnected to another box with plastic feet—surprisingly lifelike from a distance—attached to the end. My mother hadn't been able to get the blocks to click into place, and before I knew it, I was drifting across the stage. The audience started booing. Under the glare of the lights, my mother's eyes widened with panic. Her skin paled beneath her makeup. I could feel her sinking, could feel our lives sinking, like someone had weighted us down with rocks and tossed us into the ocean. When the curtain fell, I was still inside the box, and my mother still looked empty and afraid.

The first time, I didn't bring the suitcase. I didn't take anything from the shelves. I didn't even know why I was there. I just walked the aisles, gazing at the bottles and the liquids inside. It was November, but still warm and humid. I kept thinking how nice it would be to have something cold to drink.

Mr. Phillips was the only person in the store. He stood behind the counter with his paper. I was surveying a display of neon lighters near the front. I picked up a hot pink lighter and made it flame.

"It's two for one," he said without looking up. "But you look too young for those."

"I don't smoke." I put the lighter down. I didn't yet have money of my own.

"Listen to this." He tapped his index finger against the paper. I walked around to the counter. He wore a gold chain under his white T-shirt and had tufts of gray hair on his knuckles.

"A man is on his way to work, is hit in the head, and gets amnesia. He wanders away, not remembering anything, and goes on to start a whole new life. A year later, he gets his memory back, remembers where he used to live, and shows up on his family's doorstep." Mr. Phillips took off his glasses and started cleaning them on his shirt. "What a story!"

"I don't believe it," I said. "How did he get hit in the head?"

He put his glasses back on. He looked at the article again and frowned. "Well, it doesn't say exactly. But look, his picture's right here."

He passed me the paper. There was a black-and-white photo of a man with his arm around a woman. Two young girls stood in front of them. Both had braces and pigtails. Everyone was smiling. I couldn't wait to go home and tell my mother this story and ask if something like that could have happened to my father. I had no way of knowing that when I described the photo with the smiling family, she would hide her face in her hands and begin to cry.

To no one's surprise, our next show was a disaster. Backstage, Merlin hadn't wanted to get into the hat, and once he was inside, he wouldn't hold still. When my mother tilted the hat toward the audience, a white ear peeked through and people snickered. A woman and her young son, the first family I'd seen in months, walked out. Bill was in the front row, holding a beer and smiling. So far he hadn't said anything, but I imagined it was just a matter of time. Beyond the lights and the audience, I could see the dinner theater owner standing by the bar, swirling a drink and shaking his head.

When my mother pulled Merlin from the hat, he leaped out of her arms and scurried around the stage for a few minutes before diving into the audience. One man— just the kind I would have liked to buy me drinks later—

shrieked and jumped out of his chair. It didn't take long
for the rest of the audience to scatter. In the end, I caught
Merlin with the help of a baby carrot and stashed him in
our dressing room. Through the closed door, I heard the
owner shouting at my mother, telling her our days were
numbered. When she came into the dressing room, she
didn't go through her usual routine. She just sat at her table, her cape pooling around her knees, and stared at herself in the mirror.

It was too sad a scene. I left Merlin on the chaise and
my mother at her dressing table and went to the bar. Bill
was still there, nursing another beer and reading a pamphlet on manatees. Ricky looked at Bill and then back at
me, like *Now you're in trouble*.

"Are you stalking me?" I stood next to Bill and retied
my bathrobe sash. "Do I need to call the police?"

He looked up from the pamphlet. "I'm the one who
should be calling the police."

"I could have you murdered, you know." I leaned against
the bar and crossed my arms, trying to look worldly and
assured, which of course I was not. "I know people who do
that sort of thing."

Bill just laughed. "You're a kid. You don't know
anything."

"I know you want your wallet back. I know you carry a
picture of some stupid tree around. I know you won't go
back to your family and forget all about this like you
should."

"I had a family," Bill said. "A wife and a daughter and a little dog and a goldfish."

"Where did you come from, anyway?"

"Wisconsin."

"Appleton?" It seemed unlikely this man could be from the same place as Houdini.

"Sturgeon Bay. But I like it here, in Hollywood. I think I might stay for a while."

"Just because you like Hollywood doesn't mean Hollywood likes you."

Another man came into the bar, drunk and swaying and asking about the show. *Am I too late for the magic?* His shirt was untucked, his hair mussed. I sidled up to him and swiveled my hips and soon I was drinking old-fashioneds on his tab.

He was too drunk to be coy, to ask for a magic trick. After two cocktails, he was grabbing my ass and pulling me toward him. His wallet was one of the easiest. It was sitting at the top of his pocket and went straight up my bathrobe sleeve. There was a weird kind of intimacy to the whole thing, with Bill right there, and I'd had just enough to drink to feel invincible. No one else was around. What could he do but watch?

Quite a bit, it turned out.

"Thief!" Bill stood from his barstool. He pointed at me with the manatee pamphlet. "This woman is a thief!"

The drunk man clutched his pockets. Ricky looked up from restocking maraschino cherries and lime wedges. I slipped the wallet down my sleeve and slapped it on the bar.

"It was just a trick," I said. "You know, magic."

"Don't believe her," Bill said. "Don't you believe her at all."

"Thief!" the man slurred.

"Looks like the show's over," Ricky said.

A good performer always knows when it's time to make her exit. I turned on my heels and ran. I went up the middle of the audience section, between the velvet curtains. The lights were off backstage. My heels clacked on the wood. I opened the trapdoor and climbed inside the space. I wedged my head between my knees and breathed in the cedar smell. I would stay there for as long as it took for everyone to go home.

As a child, I searched for my father. I would wander down to the beach, where I checked behind garbage cans and underneath picnic tables and white lifeguard stations. Once, a lifeguard found me questioning sunbathers about my father and made me promise to go straight home. I did as I was told, but came back the next day. It was summertime. I was ten. For my birthday, my mother had given me a map of Florida, which she said would keep me from getting lost. I would study the highways and the lakes and the dark swampland. Could he be in Lake Istokpoga? Weeki Wachee Springs? Gatorland? The map made Florida seem vast and mysterious. All these names I had never heard before, all these places I had never been. This was before I understood that my father had disappeared in California, that he'd probably never made it this far east. The thing I remembered most from those days was the shape of the map. I thought Florida looked like an upside-down L.

My mother and I were awoken by a call in the middle of the night. The phone was in the kitchen, but its ring was as shrill as an alarm. I found her facing the fire escape, wearing a sleeveless cotton nightgown. The phone was pressed against her ear. She was nodding and pulling at the cord. I touched her shoulder, but she didn't seem to know I was there.

"Get dressed," she said after hanging up. "We're leaving in five minutes."

"To go where?" It was three in the morning.

My mother went into her room without answering. I pulled on jeans and a T-shirt and gathered my hair into an elastic. I forgot to put on socks before lacing my sneakers. Late last night I'd collected Merlin from the dressing room and now he was asleep on my bed. I found the leash I'd made from red silk ribbon and looped it around his neck.

In my mother's old Camaro, we drove north on Ocean Drive. The sky was dark and starless. The streetlights glowed phosphorescent white. We were heading toward Dania Beach, toward Fort Lauderdale. She rolled down the windows. Normally she listened to Donna Summer in the car, but this time the radio was silent. Merlin stood on his hind legs and sniffed the warm air.

"Will you fucking look at that?" She swerved a little when she saw him doing what we'd tried to get him to do for hours in the apartment. She hadn't taken off her makeup; mascara was smudged under her eyes and there was a halo of red around her lips. She was still wearing her black pants and white tuxedo shirt.

"Where are you taking us?"

"To the police," she said, which made me afraid to ask more questions. Had Bill reported me? Had Ricky? I slumped down in my seat and watched the buildings pass.

At the Hollywood police station, we trailed my mother through the glass doors. She asked for a Detective Swan. The station was quiet and bright and deliciously cool. Down the hall, a man was sitting on a bench, his hands cuffed behind his back.

Detective Swan was a woman, tall and broad-shouldered. Her blond hair was wrapped into a bun and stuck through with a pen. She wore a black pantsuit with a blue T-shirt underneath. She looked surprisingly alert for the hour.

"Is that a rabbit?" She pointed at Merlin.

"Does it look like a rabbit?" I held him in my arms, the leash wrapped around my hand.

My mother flicked my shoulder, her way of telling me to not be such a smart-ass.

Detective Swan led us deeper into the station. We passed the handcuffed man, who appeared to be asleep. At her desk, she pulled over two chairs and we all sat down, my mother and I side by side, the detective across from us.

"Is this your daughter?"

I felt her looking me and Merlin over. I wondered what she was seeing.

My mother nodded. "This is Crystal."

I was more certain than ever that someone had reported me, that I had overestimated the silencing power of shame. Detective Swan handed my mother a manila file folder. She opened it and stared at the contents for a while. She blinked a few times, like she had something in her eye. She wiped her nose with the back of her hand.

"That's him." She gave the folder back to Detective Swan.

"Him who?" I said.

Detective Swan asked if my mother would be willing to identify the body.

"Mom," I said, louder than I meant to. Merlin flinched in my lap. "What body?"

My mother and Detective Swan both stared at me.

"Do you want Crystal to come?" the detective asked. "We can't have a rabbit back there."

My mother leaned over and tucked my hair behind my ear. It was a tender gesture, but her eyes were not kind.

"Stay here and watch that terrible rabbit. I'll be right back."

I stood when they stood. I wanted to tell them that I was old enough to make decisions for myself, but instead I just watched as they walked down the hall.

Detective Swan had left the folder on her desk. It contained a thin stack of paper and two photos: a mug shot of a man and another from the morgue. I had never seen a dead body before, not even a picture of one. His skin looked blue and rubbery. I balanced the open file on my knees and kept reading. Merlin nibbled the edge of the folder.

Knowledge is a curious thing. People talk about realizations coming in jolts and flashes, but this was more like a gradual creeping. I imagined a water stain on a ceiling, the way it darkens and swells before it starts spreading. The man's face—the angular jaw, the sleek dark hair, the flared nose—was familiar because it was the face my mother had been describing for years. The face she claimed to have seen for the first time at magic school, in a conjuring class. She even drew it for me once, on a magic chalkboard that disappeared its drawings as soon as they were complete. Also: he had the same arch in the eyebrow, the same dimple in the cheek, that I saw in the mirror every morning and night.

Here was what I made of the evidence: there had been no magic school. No cockatoo or hypnosis. My father had never been anyone's protégé, had never been the Great

Heraldo. He had not disappeared from a water-filled aquarium. His name was Derrick Gibson and he lived in North Miami Beach and he had been shot outside a Chinese takeout at midnight.

In the car, I tried to get my mother to answer my questions. Was the dead man really my father? Had he always lived in Florida? Had they ever even set foot inside a magic school? She held the steering wheel with both hands. The heat had turned the mascara into little black puddles under her eyes.

"We did meet in California," she said as we turned back onto Ocean Drive. "Once we took a tour of a magic school in Hollywood. They had a theater filled with beautiful chandeliers and red silk draperies. I thought it was the most beautiful place I'd ever seen."

"How did you get into magic if you didn't go to the school?" It was close to dawn. The sky was pale with light.

"I took a free class once," she said. "At a community center." She had been trained by a woman who made a living doing tricks with cards and dollar bills at children's birthday parties.

My eyes were watering. Merlin felt heavy on my lap. I was breathing, but not holding on to any air. "Why did you tell so many lies?"

For that, she had no answer.

She pulled over onto the side of the road and got out of the car. She left her door open and the engine running. I followed. Merlin stayed in the passenger seat. A part of me couldn't help but admire the way he'd rejected our life choices, the way he had taken one look at us and known he didn't want to be part of this act, of this family.

"Your father came to a show once." She rolled up the sleeves of her tuxedo shirt. "About a year ago." She'd glimpsed him in the back of the theater, but by the time she looked up from her next trick, he was gone. I wondered why I hadn't known he was there, hadn't felt something inside me shift. Why he had seen me onstage and decided not to stay.

"Why did you bother telling me any of this?" In the distance, I could hear waves coming and going. "Why didn't you just keep lying?"

My mother said soon I would be eighteen, no longer a child, and she could see me daydreaming about magic and Hollywood.

"People have to be realistic about their options, Crystal."

I asked if she was being realistic about her options when she decided to be a professional magician, the most impractical fucking job anyone had ever heard of? Or when she bought the five-hundred-dollar guillotine or the rabbit? Or when she didn't like the way her life had turned out and decided to just make up a new one?

My mother told me it was time to go home.

"It won't be our home for long," I said.

She rattled the keys in her hand, then went back to the car.

At the apartment, she locked herself in the bathroom. I sat on my bed and tried to explain to Merlin what had happened. The more I told him, the angrier I became. Angry at her for wanting me to know the truth, but not telling me herself. Instead she had left the evidence in plain view, knowing I would put it all together. Angry at her for building us a life, a history, out of smoke and air. And angry at myself, because wasn't I too old to believe in stories?

When I left the theater, it was six in the morning. I stepped around broken glass on the sidewalk and a woman sleeping on a bench in an overcoat, even though it was already ninety degrees. As I walked, I looked for Bill and imagined all the men I had ever robbed filling the dinner theater like ghosts.

At Coco Cabana, I did not have my briefcase. I was just hoping for some luck. Mr. Phillips wasn't at the counter. I went to the back and wedged three mini-bottles under the waistband of my jeans. I should have stopped there, but then two little whiskeys went into my front pocket. Two more in my bra. I couldn't keep myself from plucking bottles off the shelves.

I felt hands on my back, right as I was reaching for a miniature gin. I turned and found Phillips Jr. squeezing my shoulders. He wore pressed khakis and a white polo. He smelled of cheap cologne. His hair was combed in a center part. I tipped my head back and smiled.

"Don't even try it," he said. "My father has no business sense. And he thinks you're cute, with that briefcase. That's the only reason he's let you get away with this for so long." He let go of my shoulders. He stepped back and stared at the bulges in my jeans and under my shirt. "But even he would think this is ridiculous."

Phillips Jr. took me behind the counter and told me to stay put. He dialed a number on his cell phone. Maybe the handcuffed man would still be at the police station and together we could wait for my mother to come. Maybe she would take me in her arms and apologize for all the lies. Or maybe she would decide I was just like my father and, in the years to come, tell people stories about her daughter, Crystal, who disappeared into thin air one night, in the middle of a show.

After he hung up, Phillips Jr. brought me coffee in a foam cup. For a moment, I thought he might be softening his position, but it was clear from the way he stood by the door, phone still in hand, that he thought it was time for me to learn about consequences.

"You don't have any doughnuts, do you?" Suddenly I was starving. I hadn't eaten since lunch the day before. "Like a bear claw?"

"What kind of question is that?" He shook his head. Wing-shaped sweat marks darkened the back of his polo. "This isn't a Seven-Eleven."

A small fan stood on the counter. I leaned into the breeze. Once, I took a poetry class in school and even though I hadn't been very good at writing poems, some of my similes came rushing back: time is like a house on fire; time is like water draining from a tub. I heard faraway sirens and started to worry about Merlin. If I went to jail, who would take care of him?

The door jingled, but it wasn't a police officer: it was Bill, slouching and bleary-eyed. He was wearing the same clothes from the last time I saw him. His hair clung to his scalp. His ring was gone. My father could have been a man like this, I kept thinking.

"Well," he said, sauntering over to the counter. "Look who it is."

"Do you know her?" Phillips Jr. asked.

He rocked back on his heels. "I'm sorry to say that I do."

"We're waiting on the police and she just asked for a snack. Can you believe it?"

"Nothing would surprise me." Bill picked up a six-pack and paid in cash. He asked Phillips Jr. if he could hang around for a while. He said what was about to happen would be too good to miss.

"What's your real name?" I asked Bill, who of course didn't know that all this time I'd been thinking of him as Bill. "Why did you carry around a picture of that tree?"

"It looked alive," he said.

"Of course it's alive," I said. "But why else?"

"Crystal," he said, popping open a beer. "What are you doing with your life?"

Here was another story my mother told me: once, my father hypnotized her and walked her up to the top of their apartment building in Toluca Lake. When he brought her out, she was standing on the edge of the roof. She blinked, cupped a hand over her eyes. She saw Hollywood in the distance, the sidewalk below. She felt an unfamiliar breeze, the sensation of her stomach dropping. *What am I doing here?* she asked, stepping back toward safety. *Don't worry*, he said. *I wouldn't have let you fall.* For years, I had believed the story demonstrated the power of his magic.

In the 1800s, Robert-Houdin dazzled all of Paris by casting a spell over his son that made him float. William Lance Burton conjured doves from his sleeves that perched on the shoulders of audiences. If David Copperfield could vanish the Statue of Liberty, couldn't I make just one of these bottles disappear?

"Listen." I took a whiskey out of my front pocket and placed it on the counter. "If I can make this disappear right now, before your very eyes, will you let me go?"

Phillips Jr. laughed. He looked at Bill, who raised his beer and shrugged.

"It's a deal," he said.

I closed my eyes. My feet were sweating. I curled my toes inside my sneakers. With my hands I made a circle around the bottle and tried to feel the workings of every nerve, every cell, every membrane. I tried to bring that energy upward, into my mind, where I was willing the bottle to disappear. Oh, how wonderful it would be to look at Bill, at Phillips Jr., and say: *See what I can do.*

I kept my breathing deep and slow. My fingertips burned. My hands were shaking. I had never concentrated so hard before. I heard voices ask if I was okay, and I felt myself whisper, *My father is not a magician; my father is dead.* All of it sounded very far away. I saw Merlin sitting on the theater stage, his nose twitching. I saw my mother aiming her wand at him and saying *Shazam!* I saw my father in an aquarium, his hands pressed against the glass, feeling weightless and free. I saw the bottle dematerializing with a faint hiss and a puff of smoke. I saw myself vibrate and glow before all my particles scattered like pollen in the air.

# THE ISLE OF YOUTH

# 1.

I arrived at my sister's apartment just before the hurricane. My plane had been one of the last to land at the Miami airport. From the taxi, I saw banks of black cloud settling on the horizon and palm trees bent from the wind. Bushes flapped like invisible hands were shaking them. The roads into downtown were empty. On the radio, a reporter said the hurricane would skim the coast before spinning into the Gulf of Mexico, that it would all be over by morning. I didn't believe him. The sky looked frightening. I'd never been to Florida before. My sister, Sylvia, and I were identical twins. I had not seen her in over a year.

"Does the hurricane have a name?" I asked the driver as we rolled down Sixth Street, scanning apartment buildings for the address I'd been given.

"They're always named after women," he said.

This wasn't true. I remembered Hurricanes Andrew and Floyd, but figured he was trying to make a statement.

He parked in front of my sister's building. It was tall and made of bright orange stucco. I paid the driver and got out, pulling my carry-on behind me. In the front lobby and in the elevator, the lights buzzed and flickered.

When Sylvia opened the door, I didn't enter right away. She looked like me and she didn't look like me. She had the same dainty nose and rounded chin, but she was thinner and had better posture. She had a ring in her bottom lip and carefully styled bangs. Sweatpants, a sheer white tank top, pink socks. Chipped black polish on her nails. I had no idea what my sister was doing for work. I was a research librarian and lived in D.C. My suits were poly-blend, and I hadn't been to a hair salon in months. When my sister asked me to come, I had not considered our many differences. She said it was an emergency and I told her that I had some vacation days saved. I didn't tell her that my husband and I were on the brink, and I'd been looking for something to take a chance on.

"Sylvia," I said. "How are you?"

"Looks like you brought the weather with you." She opened the door wider.

Inside, unlit candles sat on top of the coffee table and the stereo and on the ledges of bookcases. I squeezed my suitcase handle, taking in everything: the sectional sofa and flat-screen TV to my left, the kitchen to my right, the balcony with sliding glass doors, legions of candles. Even with the lights on, the apartment was dim, the storm having brought on a premature night.

"Is that safe?" I pointed to the bookcases. "To have candles so close to all that paper?"

She shut the door. "You'll thank me when the electricity goes out."

I asked my sister what I should do with my luggage. She pointed to a hallway past the kitchen. The guest room was empty, save for a futon bed, and had been converted into a storage space for musical equipment: a guitar, amps, stacks of records. I had to clear away cords and a plastic box of guitar picks to find the mattress.

I found Sylvia on the balcony. I stood beside her and looked out at the empty streets and the windblown palm trees and the distant gray swirl of ocean.

If someone were to ask about my sister, I would say she was a dangerous person. The signs started showing in junior high, when she sent a neighborhood boy, who was in love with her, into a catastrophic depression by sleeping with him and then his best friend. At thirty-four, she had been through three fiancés, countless jobs and cities and hair colors. Bankruptcy. Names. *Call me Lisa Anne*, she said one time. *Call me Suzette*, she said another. It wasn't just that my sister behaved badly—she was a shape-shifter, someone who bounced from one life to the next like a drug-resistant virus changing hosts. The longer I went without seeing her, the more comfortable I had become with the idea that she simply didn't exist, that I had no other half, no shadow self. But, after all those years, there she was, there she undeniably was, reaching for me at a time when I already felt like throwing myself under the rails.

"What's with all the music stuff in the bedroom?"

"I used to be in a band," she said. "But you wouldn't know about that."

"No, I wouldn't."

"We'll have to board these up soon." She pointed at the sliding doors behind us. "In case the glass breaks."

"Is this going to be a bad one?"

"A Category Two," she said. "Small potatoes around here."

I crossed my arms on top of the railing. "What's this hurricane named?"

"I've named her Marie Antoinette," she said. "The weather people call it something else."

"Marie Antoinette? As in let them eat cake?"

"More like off with their heads."


The power went out at nine. We had already boarded the doors; I'd held small sheets of plywood across the glass while my sister pounded in the nails. When the apartment went dark, Sylvia started lighting the candles. She did it effortlessly, as though she had practiced walking around her apartment blindfolded.

"That's it," she said. "Not much to do now but wait it out."

I sat on the couch, facing the bookcase filled with blazing candles. Rain and wind lashed the building. My sister stood in front of me and swayed. The ring in her lip glowed.

"Will you need to call Mark?" she asked. "Sometimes the reception is spotty during a storm."

"It doesn't matter," I said.

"I take it things aren't so good at home?"

I looked up at her. "How would you know?"

"I've called a few times in the last month," she said. "You weren't around. Mark brought me up to speed."

I took one of the decorative pillows and tossed it across the room. It grazed Sylvia before hitting the floor. The last time my sister visited, she and Mark went out together one night, while I was working late. They came home drunk and vicious. They sought me out in the kitchen, where I was going through my day planner, and mocked me about everything from my thick-heeled pumps (Like a witch's shoes!) to my habit of grinding coffee every night before bed (Look who's so organized! So grown up!). Even after I left the room, my sister showed no mercy. She knew how to turn people, how to get someone to abandon loyalties, to change sides. She should have gone into espionage.

"And what did Mark say?"

"He said the marriage counselor suggested you take a vacation together."

"He told you we were seeing a counselor?"

"He said she has this really annoying habit of saying 'you see' before making a point. Like 'You see, you're misdirecting your anger again,' or 'You see, now is a time for compassion.'" Sylvia sat on the floor and pulled her legs underneath her. "Where do you think you'll go for this vacation?"

"We don't know." I couldn't help but feel, through these secret conversations with my husband, that my sister had gained a kind of power over me. "Did Mark sound like he wanted to go away with me?"

"He said he was on the fence."

"We're on the fence about a lot of things."

She asked if I wanted to hear a song she'd recorded with her old band. I nodded, trying to imagine my husband standing somewhere in our house and listening to my sister's voice on the other end of the line.

Sylvia slipped a CD into the stereo, battery-operated, on hand for the storms. When the song came on, I recognized it as the one we had danced to many years ago, when we were college students, and felt an awful pang.

"Sylvia," I said. "That's David Bowie."

"Wrong track," she said. "It's a mix." She pressed a button and turned up the volume. A woman's voice overwhelmed the room. It was hollow, stretched thin, the words so elongated I couldn't understand the lyrics. An electric guitar kicked in, then drums. Sylvia tapped her fingers against her thighs, bobbed her head. The woman's voice grew shrill. I heard tambourines, another electric guitar. The song ended with the crash of cymbals.

"Which part were you?" I asked.

"The singer," she said.

The woman singing had sounded nothing like my sister.

"You don't believe me?"

"I didn't say that."

"Fine," she said. "I'll play you another."

The next song opened with rapid-fire guitar and drums, breathless lyrics. I put my hands over my eyes and listened. *I haven't seen her in ages*, I told myself. *How would I know what her singing voice was like?* But the more I listened, the more I knew it wasn't her.

I uncovered my eyes. Sylvia was dancing, in her sweatpants and socked feet and transparent shirt. The candles cast strange shadows onto her face; I could see the outline of her breasts. She raised her arms, and I caught the glint of the belly-button ring. She opened her mouth wide and words came out, her voice clashing with the singer on the stereo. Was this me in another life, me in an alternate ending? I'd heard stories about twins having secret languages and dreaming the same dreams, but I had no idea if my sister was happy or sad or terrified. She turned the volume even higher. The candles flickered. The apartment was hot.

"Sylvia," I shouted over the noise. I tried again and again. Finally I got up and put my face close to her face and called her name.

"What?" she screamed back.

"Why am I here?"

My sister told me that she wanted to change identities. I wouldn't have to do much, just show up for her job at the Bortaga, a club on Miami Beach, and hang around the apartment for a few days. Sylvia explained this to me after she'd turned off the music and sat back down on the floor. I was still on the couch, studying her face as she spoke. There was a man. He was married. She'd been having an affair with him for the last year. His wife, suspicious, had hired a private detective, who had taken photographs. Once the wife knew what Sylvia looked like and where she lived, she'd started following her. Sylvia would leave her building and see this woman parked on the street, or look over her shoulder while on the sidewalk and spot the woman behind her. She had followed Sylvia to work, the grocery, the park, the post office, the beach, the hardware store, the hair salon. My sister and the married man had decided to end things, but they wanted one last fling. He wanted to take her to the Isle of Youth, an island off the coast of Cuba, Isla de la Juventud in Spanish. There were stories about the isle being a sacred area, a place that hurricanes always missed, a place on the right side of luck.

"But you can't leave because you have this woman following you," I said. "And if you and her husband are gone at the same time, she'll never believe he's away on business or whatever he plans to tell her."

"Bingo," Sylvia said.

"I didn't see anyone loitering outside your building," I said. "I didn't see any suspicious cars."

"I hope she's not deranged enough to stalk me during a hurricane," my sister said.

"When were you planning to leave for this Isle of Youth?"

"Tomorrow night, if I can get you on board."

"Will the airport be open by then?"

"It'll be open before noon," she said. "We know how to recover quickly."

I heard a loud crash outside. A candle on the coffee table went out.

"You won't be able to wear the clothes you brought," Sylvia said. "You'll have to take things from my closet while I'm gone."

"What are you doing for work?"

"Stamping hands at a nightclub. One of those 'in the meantime' things."

I stood and walked over to the boarded-up doors. "There's no way I could pass for you in a nightclub."

"A comprehensive makeover is in order," Sylvia said. "Hair, makeup, clothes. The way I'll send you home will do more for your marriage than any romantic getaway."

"Speaking of Mark, what am I supposed to tell him?"

"That you've decided to extend your stay. That we're

helping the city of Miami with hurricane cleanup. That I'm teaching you to snorkel. It doesn't matter."

All of a sudden my sister was behind me. I knew she was there, felt her heat, without turning around. "I think Mark and I have lied to each other enough," I said.

"Deception is necessary. In marriage, in life. Otherwise the world will just sandblast us away. You have to keep something for yourself."

"There's not one good reason why I should do this for you."

"Well, for one thing, you don't like where you are right now. You've been wanting a change, an escape, for a while." She put her chin on my shoulder. She touched my hair. "Here's another one: you've always wanted to know what it would be like to be me."

The makeover began at midnight. I sat on a stool in the kitchen. Sylvia placed her supplies—a makeup bag, comb, hair spray, scissors, a glass of water—on the counter. She propped a flashlight on top of the microwave, so it shone in my face. She dipped the comb in the water and picked at my hair until it hung straight. She took a few inches off my bangs and then used a white sponge for foundation, a big brush for powder and blush, little brushes for eye shadow. She tweezed my brows, pulled at the skin beneath my eyes as she smudged on black liner and laced mascara through my lashes. She used her thumb to apply red lipstick, another tiny brush for the gloss. She swept my bangs to the side with the comb and dusted them with hair spray. Through all this, we were silent, serious. By the time she finished, the candles were melting into wax stumps and the wind was still howling.

"You've got quite a collection of beauty products," I said.

"I used to work at a salon, before the band," Sylvia said. "But you wouldn't know about that, either."

She held a mirror in front of me. In the half-lit kitchen, it was like looking at myself in a carnival mirror: my face was slimmer, my cheekbones higher, my lips swollen with color, my bangs stiff with hair spray and curving over my left eye. My sister crouched beside me and squeezed her face into the frame. We looked identical. I brought my fingers to my mouth and Sylvia batted my hand away, saying I would mess up my lipstick.

She put down the mirror and kneeled in front of me. She touched my bangs, almost tenderly. "The hair's easy. Just brush your bangs to the side while you're blow-drying in the morning, then spray, spray, spray."

"How will I remember all this on my own?"

"I thought of that already," she said. "I'll write out instructions for you tomorrow." She told me there was an envelope that had everything I would need to know, from directions to the club and the names of her co-workers to the description of the woman who had been following her to lists of what she usually bought at the grocery.

"You're being very organized about this."

"I love a good scheme," Sylvia said. "I would have been a great criminal mastermind."

"What about when I'm at your job? What if I forget someone's name or make a dumb mistake?"

"People are used to me making dumb mistakes," Sylvia said. "That's the last thing that would make anyone think you're not me."

At two in the morning, the electricity came back on. We blew out the candles and turned on the lights. The apartment was a mess: wax drippings, newspaper pinned beneath the stool in the kitchen, brushes and compacts and tubes on the counter, boarded windows. Sylvia said we would worry about cleaning in the morning. She put on cotton pajamas with martini glasses printed on them and tossed me a pair with flamingos. I had brought a T-shirt and sweatpants to sleep in, but didn't protest; her pajamas were soft and smelled like perfume.

She asked if I wanted to sleep with her, like we sometimes did when we were young, when our parents were shouting at each other and we were afraid. I said okay. In her room, she cleared away a mound of clothes and yanked out a trundle bed.

"This is where I would make my boyfriends sleep when I was mad at them," she said.

We got into our beds. Sylvia turned off the light. It was hot in the bedroom. I pushed the sheets down to my waist. I could still hear tree branches slapping the building and a terrible, tearing wind.

"When the weather's nice, I have drinks on the balcony," Sylvia said. "There's vodka in the freezer. You can do that, too, if you want."

"Okay," I said. "I'll think about it."

We were quiet for a while. I couldn't relax, couldn't even think about sleep. There was an electricity in my body unlike anything I had felt in a long time.

"I jumped off that balcony once," Sylvia said. "About a year ago. I landed in the bushes. I broke two fingers. I got a concussion. I had to spend the night in the hospital."

I rolled toward her. On the wall, I saw the shadow of her raised arm. "Why didn't someone from the hospital call me?"

"I told them I didn't have any family," she said.

"I would have helped."

"I couldn't be sure, seeing as you told me to disappear the last time we talked."

She was referring to the time she phoned to say she was in love with Mark, and that she was going to tell him so, and that she thought there was a chance he was in love with her, too. I'd told her she was a sickness and I was cutting her out. After the call, I asked Mark if he was having an affair with Sylvia. He said "no" then and he said "no" later, in the office of our marriage counselor. But still I just had this feeling. Maybe it was my imagination, or maybe I wanted someone to blame. I was willing to entertain those possibilities. What I didn't understand was why I couldn't do anything more than stand around in pain.

"You told me to stay away," she said. "So I did."

A week after the balcony, Sylvia tried to hang herself in the bathroom, but the shower rod broke. She said that she didn't even go to the hospital that time. All she had to show for her efforts was a ring of bruises around her neck.

"I have the worst luck sometimes," she said.

"Some people would say you were lucky."

Neither of us said anything more, though something about my sister's breathing told me she wanted to keep talking.

"I'm glad you're here," she finally said.

I'd heard that line before, always when I was doing whatever it was that Sylvia wanted.

"It's good that you called. Thanks for the trip to beauty school."

"Maybe you'll like my life so much, you won't want to give it back."

"We'll see," I said.

# 2.

My first day as Sylvia began at dusk. From the balcony, I watched my sister slip into a taxi. All afternoon we had been looking for the woman's car, but the coast seemed clear. After Sylvia confirmed the airport was open and her rendezvous was on, a hushed phone call taken in her bedroom, we went over everything in the envelope, spreading lists of names and work schedules and addresses across the kitchen counter. She had even gotten a fake lip ring for me. It was shaped like a comma and came in a plastic baggie. She picked out an outfit for my shift at the Bortaga, a black minidress and red heels, and did my hair and makeup once more. When it was time for her to leave, we stood in the apartment doorway. I wished her luck. She put her arms around my neck and kissed my cheek. And then she was gone.

After her taxi had disappeared down the street, I went into the bathroom and stood at the mirror. My face was bruised with makeup. My bangs drooped over my eye. I wedged the lip ring on. The metal felt strange inside my mouth. I couldn't stop running my tongue over the thin silver curve. I studied the photo of Sylvia leaning against a palm tree that hung on the bathroom wall and wondered who had taken it. This man she was meeting? I stared at her toothless smile, her narrowed eyes, and tried out the same expression in the mirror.

In the kitchen, I poured a vodka on the rocks. I stood on the balcony and watched the sun drop. There was sand on the concrete floor. The air was wet and heavy. I saw palm trees that were nothing but brown stalks and sagging power lines. Everywhere there was paper and glass and spears of wood, like the aftermath of a riot. Sylvia's building made it through the storm without any damage, but others in her neighborhood, we'd heard on the news, had broken windows and leaks. I heard a rumbling and saw a street-cleaning machine inching down Sixth Street. I finished the drink. The sun was halfway below the horizon, a watery orange orb. It seemed much bigger than the sun in Washington, the heat radiating across the tops of buildings and into me.

I woke the next morning feeling groggy, as though I'd been asleep for days. I rose and showered, using Sylvia's gardenia-scented soap and her pink pumice stone. Afterward, I put on a silk bathrobe and poked around in the medicine cabinet: a nail file, red polish, an eyelash curler, makeup sponges, pills. The bottle was labeled "lorazepam," the same thing, incidentally, a psychiatrist had once given me for nerves. I would take one and be immune to anything my husband said, any argument. I opened the bottle and found all kinds: tiny blue ones, round orange ones, rectangular pink ones. I pushed them around with my index finger and took the one that looked the most familiar. I closed the medicine cabinet and watched in the mirror as the oblong pill bled white onto the pink of my tongue.

I wrapped my hair in a towel, took the bottle of polish from the cabinet, and painted my toenails on the balcony. The streets were a little cleaner. It was hotter than before. The sky looked like a wet canvas someone had smudged with their fingers. I couldn't remember the last time I had so many open days in front of me. Sylvia worked only three nights a week at the Bortaga. Her next shift was tomorrow. Today was training.

Later I moved a hairdryer over my toes until the polish hardened. I found some jeans, low-rises with holes in the knees, and a purple tank top in the bedroom. I studied myself in Sylvia's full-length mirror. My stomach wasn't as flat and my arms were paler. I taped the beauty instructions she'd left, complete with a diagram of a face drawn in blue pen, to the bathroom mirror and did my hair and makeup. I wedged the lip ring on and looked myself over. The eyeliner was too thick, the lipstick a little heavy, but not bad. A decent imitation Sylvia.

Before leaving the apartment, I picked up the grocery list and the car keys. My sister had an old Mazda Miata convertible. I was looking forward to putting the top down. In the lobby, I opened her mailbox with the tiny key she'd given me. It was empty.

Outside, the car I'd been warned about was the first thing I saw: a beige Lincoln Town Car parked next to the Mazda. As I passed, I saw a woman with shoulder-length hair and sunglasses staring through the windshield. I started the Mazda and rolled down the top. I was a little drowsy from the pill and the sun hurt my eyes. I found rhinestone-studded sunglasses in the glove compartment and put them on. I headed to the grocery on Creston Avenue. The beige Lincoln followed.

At the grocery, I parked and rolled up the convertible top. I pushed a cart toward the entrance. The woman trailed behind me, picking up a small basket inside. She kept her sunglasses on. She followed me up and down the aisles, never more than twenty or thirty feet away. In the frozen foods section, I kept an eye on her by looking at the reflections in freezer cases, like I once saw a character do in a detective movie. Her basket stayed empty. She dragged one of her ankles slightly. I went about my business and by the time I'd checked out, she was nowhere to be found.

After the grocery, I stopped at Coco's, a café on Miami Avenue. I wanted to keep practicing being Sylvia in public. The café had blue walls and a dusty black floor. A window was covered with plywood and a sign that read COCO VS. FLORA was taped to the sheets. I peered into a glass pastry case, trying to decide between a cupcake and a muffin. I went with the cupcake and a coffee because I thought that was what Sylvia would want.

"So the hurricane was named Flora?" I asked the woman behind the register. She had drawn-on eyebrows and cropped hair.

"That's what they call it on the news," she said. "I call it something else."

"What's that?"

"Magdalena. After my mother."

I took a table facing the entrance. I scraped the icing off the cupcake with a plastic knife and ate it, just like Sylvia did when we were kids. The ceiling fan moved in lazy circles. I was finishing my coffee when the woman who had been trailing me came in and sat down. When I first saw

her, I almost let the mug slip from my hands. In the grocery, she'd kept her distance. I expected her to wait on the
sidewalk or in her car. I didn't think she'd come so close.

She took the booth by the covered window, facing me.
She didn't order anything; her sunglasses were still in place.
She folded her hands on top of the table. I took my time
finishing my coffee. The last few sips were bitter and thick.

After the coffee was gone, I put my own sunglasses
back on. I was worried the woman might detect a difference in my eyes. Then I went and sat across from her. Her
brown hair was streaked with blond, her skin freckled and
tan. She smelled like coconut oil. She wore a white T-shirt
and jeans and a thick gold watch. I wondered if my sister
had even gotten this close to the woman before. I liked the
idea of being braver than Sylvia.

"What's your name?" I said.

"My husband never told you?"

"Never."

"I've been following you for a month and you've never
said a word to me." She crossed her arms, holding on to
her elbows. "Why today?"

"I want to know why you're following me."

"You know plenty."

"I want to know when you'll stop."

"I could hurt you. Right now. I really could." She
pressed her fingers against her forehead.

"I'm going to the video store next, just to give you a
heads-up," I said. "It feels like a Hitchcock kind of night."

I left her sitting in the booth. I wasn't sure she'd followed until I walked out of the video store, where I'd used my sister's card to rent *Vertigo*, and saw the Lincoln in the parking lot. I waved to the woman before driving off.

That evening, as I watched the movie on Sylvia's TV, the phone rang. I ignored it, as I imagined Sylvia would. When I heard her voice on the machine, I paused the film. She was calling to give me the number of her hotel on the Isle of Youth. She said the island was split into two sections, the north and the south, and that a large swamp ran through the center. She said it was even hotter than Miami. There were green iguanas on the rocks and black coral in the ocean and if you dove at Los Barcos Hundidos, you could see the skeletons of sunken ships. She said it felt good to be seeing different things. *Thank you*. Sylvia paused. I heard bells in the background. *I owe you big*.

For my first night at the Bortaga, I put on the outfit Sylvia had given me and prepared my hair and makeup with extra care. At dusk, I drank a vodka on the balcony. The Miami skyline was a wall of pink light. Before leaving, I took a pill. In the car, I practiced saying my name was Sylvia.

On the road, it was too dark to see if the Lincoln was following. I put the top down and let the wind roar through my hair. The bridge that led to Miami Beach was lit gold. I saw dark water below, heard music coming from party boats. My husband always said Sylvia was more fun, more freewheeling. I wondered what he would think if he was riding beside me, if he would be frightened when I hit the gas and screamed around a corner, if he would be surprised, if he would know who I was.

I took a wrong turn near Española Way and got to the club late. I touched up my lipstick in the rearview, then gave the valet my car. I walked past the line outside and the black-shirted bouncers, trying not to wobble in my heels. When I entered the club, I was hit with cold air. A stainless steel bar stretched down one side of the room; on the other, a staircase spiraled into the darkness upstairs. In the back, DJs stood on a stage and people danced beneath streams of flashing light. The lights made the dancing bodies look fragmented and strange.

I walked up to the woman sitting on a black stool and stamping the hands of people entering. She was pixieish and scowling. Her silver dress showed the dragon tattooed on the tops of her breasts. Her name was Lydia, according to my sister's notes.

"Sorry I'm late," I said.

"You're always late." She jammed the inkpad and stamp into my hands, then drifted over to the bar, where she sat for a minute before disappearing into the mass on the dance floor.

My sister was right about one thing. Her job was easy. The people knew to stick out their hands, palms down; all I had to do was press on the phosphorescent stamp. I listened to the music. I thought about Sylvia on the Isle of Youth, with the black coral and the iguanas. I imagined my husband watching the news in our living room. He liked to turn all the lights off when he watched TV. He felt so far from me, now that I had slipped into this other dimension, this crack in the earth. All the questions that had plagued me on the flight to Miami—Does he want me to stay? To go?—felt remote, like background noise.

I'd been stamping hands for an hour when I spotted the woman who had been following me. She wore a dress with a scoop neck and long sleeves, which looked out of place in the sea of naked bellies and shoulders and thighs. In the line, she looked straight ahead and held out her hand. I rolled on the stamp.

"Won't your husband wonder where you are?" I whispered.

"He could care less."

She went to the bar. The bartender brought her a drink without being asked. She didn't seem to be watching me very closely, which I took to mean she'd been to the Bortaga enough times to know what my sister did.

I was looking at the woman when I felt a hand on my shoulder. A man in a gray suit stood over me. His hair fell to his chin and his eyes were different colors, one of them blue, the other hazel. He leaned down and pressed his lips against my ear.

"Meet me upstairs in five," he said.

He went up the spiral staircase, vanishing into the dark-

ness above. I was gazing upward when a bouncer called
my sister's name and pointed at the small group waiting
for me to stamp their hands. I spotted Lydia and waved
her over. Sweat had beaded on her temples.

"I need you to cover me," I said, handing her the inkpad
and stamp.

On the staircase, I put my hand on the cool steel railing and started to climb. What had my sister failed to tell
me? It could be anything. That I knew.

At the top of the stairs, there was a dark hallway with
doors at each end. I could tell from the flat sheets of light
shooting through the bottoms. The growl of heavy metal
came from behind one of the doors. The man in the gray
suit was waiting in the shadows, leaning against a wall. I
stood next to him. My palms were damp. I felt on the
verge of being exposed. Up close, would I sound like my
sister, smell like my sister? I was grateful for the darkness.

He moved in front of me and put his hands on my
shoulders. He asked if I had it.

"It?"

"What we discussed."

"Yes," I said. "I mean, I will."

"Sylvia." He moved his hand over my face, closing my
eyes. Then his fingers went down my stomach. I leaned
into the wall, unsure if I was supposed to be frightened or
enthralled.

He said my sister's name again. I asked what he wanted.
I kept my eyes closed.

"I need to know that you'll be there," he said.

"There?"

He pulled his hand away. "Don't act stupid. It doesn't become you."

"Okay," I said. "I'll be there."

"With what we discussed?"

"Right. With what we discussed."

He stepped back. "I don't want to see anything happen to you, Sylvia."

"I know," I said. "Of course not."

He touched my neck, his fingers pressing into the little dip at the base, before walking down the hall and disappearing behind a door. When I went downstairs, into the blistering light, the ceiling was raining silver confetti.


At Sylvia's apartment, I took the cordless phone onto the balcony and called her hotel. The front desk transferred me to her room and when she didn't answer, I left a message. I told her about the gray-suited man, that she was supposed to have something for him, that some kind of meeting had been arranged. I said she had to tell me what was going on, that this wasn't the kind of thing I could pretend my way through. I said she was wrong about what she'd told me earlier, that I hadn't agreed to this because I wanted to know what it was like to be her. *Couldn't you see,* I said, *that I just wanted to get out of my life?*

The sky was black, the horizon electric. I heard the distant whoosh of the ocean. Even at night, the heat was crushing. I leaned over the railing and stared at the sidewalk. Cars lined the street; people drifted up and down the concrete strip. I tried to imagine Sylvia flinging herself over the iron barrier and dropping through the air like a meteor. Her apartment was only on the third floor. Thick hedges bordered the sidewalk; the lawn was green and soft. Certainly it was possible for someone to jump off the balcony and survive. I wondered what those first waking moments, on the grass or in the hedges, might have been like for Sylvia. I wondered, as I lived my own unhappy life hundreds of miles away, if any of those sudden, inexplicable pains—the ache in the belly, the cramp in the knee—was some primitive part of my brain registering that my other half was in peril.

I went into the living room and dialed my husband's number. We hadn't spoken since I phoned to say I was extending my stay in Miami. But, I realized as the phone rang, I didn't have to be the person calling him now.

"Mark," I said when he answered, adopting my sister's higher pitch. "It's Sylvia."

"How's the weather?" he asked. "The storm?"

"It's passed."

"And my wife?"

"She's fine," I said. "A bit difficult at times."

He paused. I thought I heard a door close. "Sylvia would

never say 'a bit difficult.' She would say 'she's a pain in the ass' or 'she's fucked in the head.' She wouldn't be delicate about it."

"You got me." My voice slipped back to its usual tone. I lay on the floor, my legs stretching underneath the coffee table.

"Why would you pretend to be Sylvia?" he asked. "After all you've been through with her?"

"You mean after all *we've* been through with her."

"When are you coming home?"

I nestled the phone between my chin and shoulder. "Soon. When Sylvia is done needing me."

"Since when do you care about Sylvia needing you?" he said. "I don't understand why you went down there in the first place, let alone why you're staying."

"Since when do you have conversations with my sister without telling me?"

"It's not what you think."

"How would you know what I think?"

He was quiet for a moment. "Let's not let this go the way it always goes."

I picked at the wax drippings that had solidified on the carpet. "When I get back, are we going to take that trip or what?"

"Yes," he said. "We'll do it."

"You really want to?"

"I really do."

"Sylvia said you weren't sure."

"Sometimes we get frustrated. Sometimes we say things we don't mean." He sighed. "I don't know what else to tell you."

"So much," I said. "There's so much more you could tell me."

"I've decided I want to go away with you," he said. "Can't we just leave it at that?"

"That's been our whole problem. Deciding to leave things at that."

"You're making it impossible to talk."

"Fine. Where will we go? Tell me." I listened to his breath on the line.

"One summer, when I was in college, I visited a Tibetan monastery," he said. "It was just outside of Lhasa. I sat in silence with the monks for three days. We could do something like that, something spiritual."

I already knew about this trip. He'd taken it in the company of his former girlfriend, whom he'd come close to marrying, but I didn't bring that up. His voice reminded me of who I really was, of the deepness of my—our—unhappiness. When you're married, our counselor had told us, happiness is like a joint banking account; it becomes full or depleted in tandem.

"I was thinking an island might be nice," I said.

"I hate to swim. You know that about me."

I rested the phone against my chest. My husband started talking about practical things, how long we could afford to stay away, whether or not we should use a travel agent or buy insurance. His voice passed over me like wind.

# 3.

The next morning, when I went into the kitchen to make coffee, I found two men sitting on the living room sofa. They stood and introduced themselves as A2 and B2. They were broad-shouldered and bald. They both had round faces and squinty eyes. They wore black T-shirts and black slacks and boots. They told me that my name was no longer Sylvia Collins. To them, I was only the mark: C2.

I hadn't done my makeup or hair or put on the lip ring. I was naked underneath my sister's silk bathrobe. I crossed my arms over my chest.

"What's with the names?" I said.

"It's the Pythagorean theorem," A said. "We used to be mathematicians."

"You missed your meeting this morning," B said, stepping closer to me. "You told Andre you'd be there and you weren't. So we've been sent to keep an eye on you, to make sure you're getting things in order, like you've told people you would."

"And to make sure you don't split," A said.

I sat on the floor. My bathrobe gaped open. The whole picture was coming into focus, a blur in my periphery gradually taking shape, like when your sight starts recovering after getting eyedrops at the doctor's office. I pressed my legs together. I felt like I was sinking into the floor.

"This is a complicated situation," I said.

"Everyone tells us that," A said.

"Sylvia isn't here right now. I mean, I'm not actually Sylvia."

"Everyone tells us that, too," B said.

I asked about making a call. The men shrugged. I dialed my sister's hotel room and got the machine again. I told her that two men were in her apartment and she needed to take the next flight home. After hanging up, I turned to A and B, who were unimpressed.

"Listen," A said. "Nothing is going to happen to you. Not yet. It's too soon for that sort of thing, we've been told."

"Just do what you've promised to do," B said.

"I didn't promise anything," I told them. "I'm not Sylvia."

"Whatever," they said.


I made coffee and got dressed, taking the first thing I saw in the drawer: jean shorts and a red tube top. In the bathroom, I styled my bangs and did the makeup basics— lipstick, mascara, blush—and put on the lip ring. When I came back into the kitchen, A and B had emptied the coffeepot. They took up too much space in the apartment. I needed to get out.

I drove to Coco's with A and B in the backseat. Before leaving, I'd taken one of Sylvia's pills, and when they realized what I was up to in the bathroom, they'd demanded a dose of their own. These kinds of jobs have their perks, A had said, knocking his back without any water. In the car, they squabbled over radio stations.

"Are all people in your profession like this?" I asked.

"Like what?" they said.

We passed high-rises and surf shops, snow-cone vendors and hot-dog stands. There was little sign of the storm by then, just the occasional ripped billboard or bare palm tree. In the rearview, I saw the Lincoln behind us. I rolled down the window and waved.

"Who are you waving to?" A wanted to know.

"No one," I said.

"Is this a convertible?" B asked.

I nodded.

"Put down the top," he said.

"I don't feel like it."

A leaned over the console. His cologne reminded me of what my father used to wear. He had a silver stud in his ear. I felt his breath on my neck.

"Who gives a fuck what you feel like?" he said.

I put the top down. Wind raked through my hair. The breeze felt good. At a red light, I took my hands off the wheel and thrust my arms into the open air.

———

At Coco's, A and B took a table in the corner and waited. The window was still boarded up. The boy behind the counter had a black eye. Ants crawled beneath the plastic dome covering a lemon meringue pie. While I was in line, the woman came in and took the same booth. She wore her sunglasses. A little orange scarf was tied around her neck. I got my coffee and joined her. This time, I kept my sunglasses off.

I touched the boards covering the window. "I wonder how much longer these will be here."

"Who knows," she said. "We're used to seeing the mark of storms."

"Don't you want something to eat?" I asked. "Something to drink?"

She shook her head. I asked what she knew about the Isle of Youth.

"Many years ago, I went there with my husband," she said. "It was full of marshes and huge insects. The houses and hotels were falling in. It was anything but a paradise."

"I don't know your husband, but he isn't on a business trip, like he said."

She took off her sunglasses. Her eyes were a dull blue. "What are you talking about?"

I looked past the woman, at A and B, who were huddled together at their table, watching. "I'm not sure how to explain this," I began, and then I told her everything. That it was my sister, Sylvia, and not me, her twin, having the affair, that I was just filling in while they had one last hurrah. And now, thanks to my sister's involvement in God-knows-what, I was being followed by two men who wouldn't believe me when I said I wasn't her.

The woman cupped a hand over her eyes. "My husband hasn't left town, on business or otherwise, since April."

"What?"

"He lost his job," she said. "I thought you knew about that."

"When did you see him last?"

"This morning. I watched him do a crossword puzzle. He kept asking if I knew a synonym for 'flummoxed.'"

"You mean he's home? Right now?"

"Yes," she said. "Right now."

On the radio, I caught the end of one of the songs Sylvia had played for me and claimed as her own. My cheeks tingled. I leaned back in the booth and tried to picture my next step.

"Why do you even believe me?" I asked. "I mean, how do you know I'm not Sylvia?"

"You walk like you're not sure where you want to go. You're nervous, unsure. Your sister acts like she has nothing but ice inside her."

I felt relieved that there might be a way to tell us apart after all.

"Why would you do this for someone?" the woman asked. "Why would you agree to take over her life?"

I considered telling her that I had wanted to help my

sister, that I had wanted us to reconnect, even though that wasn't it at all. I had always thought of Sylvia as being free—of responsibility, of decency, of career and home, of building the things you're supposed to build, the things that everyone says are so important.

"I wanted to feel free," I said.

"I don't know why I've done what I've done." The woman shook her head. "Why I didn't just leave."

"I could say the same thing."

"Where are these men?" She leaned toward me. "The ones who are following you."

"Sitting behind you."

She nodded, but didn't look over her shoulder. I admired her restraint.

"What are you going to do about them? Should you call the police?"

"I don't think it works that way." I stood up. I had the number for Sylvia's hotel in my purse. I looked down at the woman, then over at A and B. The only time my husband ever followed me was on our second wedding anniversary. He waited outside the library and trailed me to the park where I usually ate lunch. I was unwrapping a tuna sandwich when he appeared from behind a tree, holding a white box with a cake inside. Flash forward five years, and he'd stopped chasing after me when I stormed out during our fights. As I looked at the three faces of my followers, I was hit with something almost like desire.

I headed for the door. The men followed. The woman did not.

I went to a pay phone down the street, A and B in pursuit. I fished some quarters from my purse and dialed Sylvia's number. She answered after one ring.

"Hello," I said. "It's me." The sky was bright. I put on the sunglasses.

"Oh," she said. "I thought you were going to be someone else."

"So here's what I know: your lover is home, in Miami, and you're in deep shit. Two men have been sent to keep an eye on you because you missed some kind of meeting." A was leaning against a telephone pole. B was rolling a little gray rock around on the sidewalk with the toe of his boot.

"I needed you." She was quiet for a moment. "You wouldn't have agreed to fill in for me if you knew what I was really doing."

"Which is?"

"Correcting a supply problem."

"You cannot be serious."

"A and B are harmless. They're never sent to do the dirty work."

"This is more than I can handle," I said. "This is more than I agreed to. Are you even on the Isle of Youth?"

"That part's true," she said. "But it's not what I thought it would be like. It's dirty and run-down."

"This trip hasn't been what I thought it would be like either," I said. "Not even close."

"I'm still coming back when I promised," she said. "I'll meet you at the apartment tomorrow night. Everything will get straightened out then."

"As soon as you walk through the door, I'm gone."

"You don't care about what happens to me?"

"You said everything would get straightened out."

"Wouldn't you want to be sure?"

I didn't say anything.

"Change of subject. What's my life like these days?"

"Lonely," I said. "Very lonely."

"Tomorrow night." She inhaled sharply, as though she was about to say something else, then hung up the phone.

"See?" I said, turning to the men. "I'm not Sylvia. I'm her sister. I was just talking to Sylvia on the phone."

"Bravo," A said.

"Nice show." B applauded.

"You two should have stuck with math," I said as we walked back to the car.

I drove around downtown Miami in a daze. The sky was clear; it was hard to believe a hurricane had blown through only a few days before. We kept the top down. A and B were bickering over the radio again. They finally agreed on NPR.

"We like *The Infinite Mind*," B told me. This week's program featured a woman who, after brain surgery, woke up believing she was a nineteenth-century monk. Formerly a fifth-grade English teacher, the woman now recited details of her ascent through the order and her life in the monastery, all of which checked out with religious scholars. Soon her speech and motor skills began to decline, and the last word she spoke was *megaloschemos*, Greek for "great schema," a term used for a monk who had reached the highest level of spiritual enlightenment.

After the program ended, B said the story illustrated how speech is an inauthentic form of communication.

"Think about it," he said. "She reached, symbolically speaking, the highest level of enlightenment just before she stopped talking."

A countered that it was a commentary on inborn knowledge, on how we hold inside ourselves ideas and experiences that exist on a plane far above our conscious minds.

"For example," he said, "the first time someone asked me to take a gun apart and put it back together, I did it automatically, even though I'd never been taught how. I'd been holding this knowledge inside me without knowing it."

"Maybe it's a commentary on how badly this woman's surgeon fucked up," I said.

"That's just cynicism," A said. "That's too easy, too shallow."

"To look away from mystery is to look away from life itself," B added.

"Jesus Christ," I said. "Why are you talking like that?"

"It's what distinguishes us in our profession," B said. "Our thoughtfulness."

We passed kids riding low-slung bicycles and a bus full of nuns. I wondered what kind of inborn knowledge I might have inside me. I imagined a silver spiral sitting in my chest, waiting to be utilized. I had just turned onto Eleventh Street when the men began to criticize my driving.

"You're just driving around the same blocks," B said. "You should be getting it together, sorting things out."

"I don't know where to go," I said. "I don't know what to do."

"Figure something out," A said. "We're getting bored back here."

I steered the car toward the one place I knew my sister stayed away from.

Sylvia never liked water. When we were twelve, our parents took us on a trip to Carmel. At night, in our resort room with dolphin-printed wallpaper, my sister was kept awake by nightmares about being swept out to sea. I had enjoyed the trip because it was one of the few times I was better at something; I swam with abandon, ducking underwater and holding my breath until I felt my lungs would burst.

After parking the Mazda on the edge of Miami Beach, I took off my sandals. A and B lumbered along behind me. The beach was a great sweep of cerulean water and white sand; when I looked into the distance, I saw the peaks of boats. Striped umbrellas jutted from the ground. Yellow and lavender lifeguard towers dotted the shore. Girls lay facedown in the sand, their bronzed backs and legs gleaming. Since leaving Coco's, there had been no sign of the woman and her beige Lincoln.

I left my sandals in the sand and went in up to my ankles. The ocean was warm. I continued until the water reached the ragged hem of my shorts. I looked back at A and B. They were standing on the beach, in the shade of a palm tree, their arms crossed. I only needed to go a little farther to feel the bottom disappear, to feel nothing but water beneath me, but I liked the firm boundary under my feet. I stared at everything that lay beyond: blueness, escape, certain death. It felt strange to know that behind me stood such an immense and troubled city.

I remembered once trying to convince my husband and Sylvia to spend a weekend at the beach, but he said he didn't like the ocean, and Sylvia looked at him and smiled and then commented on how alike they were. I had been grating carrots for a salad. I put down the grater, confused. My husband and I had gone to the Eastern Shore all the time during the early years of our marriage. I'd never known he didn't like the sea. *Since when?* I'd wanted to ask him. *What changed?* It seemed clear to me that my sister's fear had infected him.

I went back to that fear, to that seaside trip with our parents, which revealed a side of Sylvia I had never seen before: shivering, small, vulnerable. She always looked so unhappy when she emerged from the water, with her slicked-down hair and blue lips, like a cat that had been sprayed with a hose. On our last afternoon, Sylvia suggested we play a game where we held each other's head underwater, to see who could stay down longer. Her only condition was that we didn't go out past our waists. I agreed, certain I could win. Sylvia lasted twenty seconds before she pinched my leg, the signal to let go. I still remembered how slim and pale her limbs looked underneath the water, and the silken feeling of her wet hair between my fingers. When it was my turn, I made it forty seconds before running out of air, but when I pinched Sylvia's leg, nothing happened. Her hands bore down against the back of my head. I swung my arms and legs, dug my fingernails into her knee. By the time she released, I was gasping, openmouthed, like a fish stranded on land. *You didn't follow the rules*, I shouted, but she just went back to shore and ran down the beach, the shallow water spraying around her ankles, her power restored.

Clouds were thickening along the horizon; the boats had disappeared from sight. The ocean looked choppy and gray. I wanted a jolt, something that would snap me back into a world I recognized. I bent over and dunked my head into the water. The salt stung my eyes.

When the sky dimmed, I trudged out of the water and drove home. In the lobby, I checked the mailbox. There was a postcard of the Isle of Youth: a photo of a turquoise sea and a white sailboat. The back of the card had gotten wet and the ink had bled. I held it up to A and B.

"Sylvia sent me this card," I said. "She sent it from the Isle of Youth."

"I can't read the message on the back," A said.

"You could have sent that card to yourself," B added.

I put the postcard back into the mailbox, then turned to the men and asked why they weren't making me do whatever work Sylvia was supposed to be doing.

"That'll be someone else's job," A said.

In the apartment, the men asked if there was any pizza, so I ordered one. Later we ate and watched *Die Hard* on TV. After the movie, I didn't wrap the extra pizza in tinfoil and put it in the fridge, like I would have at home. I left the box on the kitchen counter, our glasses and plates and crumpled paper napkins on the coffee table.

I slipped into the bedroom, where I changed into a pair of Sylvia's pajamas and called my husband.

"It's me," I said when he answered.

"I know," he said. "You don't have to tell me."

I lay on the bed, facing the wall. "I'm in a situation."

"A situation?"

"This is going to sound like a lot to ask, but I want you to come down to Florida tomorrow night. I want you to meet me at Sylvia's apartment and take me home."

"You've never had much trouble coming and going."

"You don't know what I've been through."

"Explain it to me."

"I'm being followed by three people," I said, though my mind was already moving in a different direction entirely, back to certain times with my husband, when the fights were just starting to get dangerous, when every night, it seemed, we found ourselves on the brink of losing irretrievable ground. There were things people could say to each other that brought about a kind of death, in that you never get over it; you apologize and seek counseling, you tell people your marriage is "recovering," but you're presiding over a grave. Of course, I didn't have such ideas back then, when we still had a chance. I thought we were like rubber. I thought everything would bounce off.

"Who are these people that are following you?" my husband asked.

"Well, actually, now I think it's down to two."

"Did your sister get you stoned?"

"I haven't seen Sylvia in days." I rubbed my eyes. "She went to the Isle of Youth. It's an island near Cuba. It has black coral and iguanas."

Someone knocked on the bedroom door. I heard A's voice. He wanted to know who I was talking to.

"I have to go," I said. "Please think about what I asked you to do."

"What's that noise?"

"I can't go into it right now."

"If you think I'm going to drop everything and fly to Florida, you're nuts."

"Do you think speech is inhibiting our spiritual enlightenment?"

"What?" he huffed into the phone. "What, what, what?"

The door opened. I hung up. A and B loomed in the doorway.

"That wasn't an authorized call," A said. "I sincerely hope you weren't calling the cops."

"I didn't know I needed permission," I said. "Anyway, I was just talking to my husband."

"They told us you weren't married," B said.

"They wouldn't know." I put on a pink bathrobe and pushed past them, toward the balcony. I leaned against the railing. My hips dug into the metal. The skyline was brilliant with light.

I recalled what Sylvia said that first night in her apartment, about me wanting to know what her life was like. I turned my head from side to side, looking at the men standing next to me. "Now I know how it feels to never be alone, but in absolutely the wrong kind of way."

"We're probably no worse than most of the company you keep," B said.

"You might be right about that," I said.

I leaned over the edge of the balcony. The ground below looked dark and smooth, like the surface of another planet. I wanted to touch it, to feel the grass against my cheek. I kept leaning and leaning until I was weightless. As I went, I felt something—fingertips?—graze the bottom of my feet. I hit the lawn hard. My legs were tangled in the bushes, my arms sprawled across the grass, as though I were trying to crawl away from the scene. I wondered if this was where Sylvia had landed when she went over the edge. I pictured a chalk outline and my body filling the shape.

My lip was bleeding. I was sweating underneath my pajamas and robe. The back of my head ached. I pressed my face into the grass, not looking up when I heard footsteps or voices. I imagined A and B trying to explain this to their boss: she was there and then she wasn't.

"There is something very wrong with you," A said.

I rolled onto my back. Blood had pooled below my bottom lip. I swallowed a mouthful of liquid and grit. The sky had that smudged look again. If my husband knew I'd gone over a balcony, would he come for me then?

B kneeled next to me. He pressed two fingers against my throat.

"The good news is that you're going to live," he said.

"What's the bad news?"

They were going to have to take me back upstairs. I nodded.

"We have to keep you safe," B said. "No one will be able to make you do anything if your bones are already broken."

I nodded a second time.

"Why did you do this?" he asked.

"I had to do something."

A kneeled on my other side. He rested his palm on my forehead. "What hurts?"

In the apartment, A and B helped me down the hall and into Sylvia's bed. They put a pillow underneath my left ankle, which was already swelling. They cleaned the dirt and grass from my face and hands with a warm washcloth. Using a Q-tip, A swabbed blood from my bottom lip, then peered into my mouth.

"It's just a cut." He held out a coffee mug and I spat blood into the white bottom. "You don't need any stitches."

"I feel like I've been shot," I said.

"No, you don't." B picked leaves from my hair.

They bandaged my ankle and brought me two pills from Sylvia's supply and a glass of water. I took the pills and gulped the water like it was the last thing I would ever drink. They turned out the lights. They told me that tomorrow was a new day.

The door opened. I knew they were about to leave. I asked them to wait.

"Why did you drop out of graduate school?" I asked. "Why didn't you become mathematicians?"

"What do you care?" they said.

"I want to know something about you."

The room was dark. I blinked, trying to find their silhouettes. I listened for their voices.

"It's not a very interesting story," A said before closing the door.


I woke in the middle of the night with a violent energy inside me. I had to get out of my sister's room. I limped down the hall and locked myself in the bathroom. I padded the tub with towels and eased myself in. I pulled the shower curtain closed. I uncapped my sister's gels and shampoos and sniffed the liquids. Everything smelled like a bad imitation of something else. My elbow was bruised. My cut lip throbbed. The back of my head still hurt. I wondered if my brain was bleeding. I heard A and B snoring in the living room, where they'd taken up residence for the night.

I fell asleep in the bathtub. In the morning, I woke to the sound of A and B shouting. Finding my room empty, they thought I had slipped out of the apartment. I got up, using the tile walls for support, and splashed water on my face. There was a greenish bruise on my cheek and dried blood around my mouth. I imagined the previous day repeating itself over and over and that sick feeling returned. When I opened the door and hobbled into the living room, the men stopped yelling and stared.

"I was in the bathroom," I said.

"The bathroom?" A said. "What were you doing in there?"

"Who cares," B said. "She was just in the bathroom. We didn't lose her after all."

They looked at each other and laughed until they were red-faced and doubled over. I sat on the floor and leaned against the wall. I felt a strange pressure in my cheekbones.

"How are you feeling?" they finally asked.

"My sister is coming home tonight," I said.

"I'll put on some coffee," A said. "Looks like you need it."

I told them I wanted to make a call. They glanced at each other, then handed me the phone. I lay on my side and dialed my husband's number. I thought of the stories I'd heard about adversity bringing couples back together. When the machine came on, I repeated his name until the line went dead.

After the sun had been swallowed by a phosphorescent night, I waited on the balcony for Sylvia, a vodka sweating in my hand. My ankle was still wrapped and I couldn't put weight on it, so I stood with my foot slightly raised, like a flamingo. A and B stood with me, of course, complaining about the heat and the mosquitoes and all the trouble I had caused them.

"Who are we waiting for again?" A asked.

"My sister," I said. "The person you're really supposed to be following."

B slapped at a bug on his forearm. "Lady, has anyone ever told you that you have a reality perception problem?"

I watched the street. A car parked in the shadows resembled the Lincoln, but it was too dark to know for sure. I thought of the last fight I had with my husband. It started in the kitchen and progressed to the bedroom. In a fury, I'd climbed out the bedroom window and onto the roof. My husband stuck his head outside and called to me. I ignored him. A little while later, he walked down the driveway and got in his car. He left and didn't return until morning. I stayed on the rooftop for hours, watching the black sky. Once, a plane passed over me. I wanted badly to be on one and a few weeks later I was, bound for Miami. And even with all that had happened, with everything that had gone wrong, there was still a part of me saying, *Please don't send me back to where I came from.*

Before my sister appeared, a little black briefcase in hand, there were several false alarms—women who had the same slim silhouette, who walked with the same kind of swagger. It was startling to see how many people I mistook for my sister, stopping just short of leaning over the balcony and shouting her name; it was even more startling to realize that to mistake someone for Sylvia was to mistake them for myself, that there were so many women who, in the dark, could pass for me. And so when the real Sylvia got out of a taxi and moved like a shadow across the street, I didn't call to her. I didn't wave. Instead I remembered watching her run down that beach in Carmel, looking radiant and weightless, filling me with terror and awe.

Sylvia stood on the sidewalk, beneath a streetlamp. The light fell on her in a perfect yellow dome. She looked like she was posing for a portrait. She bowed her head. Her body heaved with a mammoth sigh. "There she is," I whispered to A and B just before she disappeared inside.

## ACKNOWLEDGMENTS

Thank you:

To the people who first supported these stories: Jill Myers at *American Short Fiction*; Susan Burmeister-Brown and Linda Swanson-Davies at *Glimmer Train*; Pei-Ling Lue and Maribeth Batcha at *One Teen Story*; Cara Blue Adams at *Southern Review*; Bradford Morrow at *Conjunctions*; Dewitt Henry and Ladette Randolph at *Ploughshares*; the Julia Peterkin Award committee; the Writer's Center.

To the Barnes & Noble Discover Great New Writers Program and the Munster Literature Centre, for helping me keep the faith.

To Spiro Arts, the Ragdale Foundation, and the Virginia Center for the Creative Arts, for the great gift of time.

To the communities at Gettysburg College, especially Fred Leebron and Kathryn Rhett; Gilman School, especially Patrick Hastings and John Rowell; George Washington University, especially Tom Mallon; and the Bread Loaf Writers' Conference, especially Michael Collier and Noreen Cargill.

To Baltimore, for being the place where so much of this work got done. To the Baltimore lit gang, the best any city could hope for.

To Joe Hall and Cheryl Quimba, for lending me 3036 Guilford, where this book was finished.

To Don Lee, Elliott Holt, Mike Scalise, Nina McConigley, Jessica Anthony, Jane Delury, Shannon Derby, and Meghan Kenny, for their faith and friendship. To Karen Russell, for her luminous e-mails and support.

To those who read early versions of these stories and helped me find my way out of the forest of the first draft: Josh Weil, James Scott, Matthew Salesses.

To my agent, Katherine Fausset, for being brilliant and loyal and fearless, always with the utmost grace. Thanks as well to Stuart Waterman and everyone else at Curtis Brown.

To my editor, the genius Emily Bell, for taking a chance on me and for shepherding these stories into their final form. To everyone at FSG who helped bring this book into existence. To Nayon Cho. To Gregory Wazowicz. To anyone who did anything to help. I will be in your debt always.

To my family, immediate and extended. To my parents, Egerton and Caroline. To CJ. Every book is for you.